My Hundred Million Dollar Secret

David Weinberger

My Hundred Million Dollar Secret

© 2006 David Weinberger

www.my100milliondollarsecret.com

ISBN 978-1-84728-800-4

Chapter 1

I can't say that Friday, April 13, was a good day even though that's when I won the lottery.

It's not that my standards are too high. It certainly wasn't a bad day. It was more like a complex day: That Friday took my simple kid's life and made it as knotty as a sweater knit by a squirrel who just got off a roller coaster.

You'd think that having money would make everything easy. If you get grass stains on your best pants, you just reach into your closet where another hundred pairs hang. If you can't decide which video game to buy, you buy them both and throw another dozen into the shopping cart…which is being pushed by your butler. But being rich had exactly the opposite effect on me. Maybe it was because I became so rich so suddenly. Or maybe it was because of the way I became rich. Or maybe it was because buying pants and video games is the easy part.

Or maybe it was because … Well, it's a long story.

● ● ●

On the Monday before that Friday the 13th, I was at the Pick-a-Chick. That's what the sign said outside, although it wasn't really a Pick-a-Chick anymore. It was Herb's This 'n That Store. I'm only thirteen, and I can name three other businesses that used to own that store. First it was McCardle's Milk, which was cool because they had Pop Gums, a slime-green ice cream bar with bubble gum in the middle of it. Then it was Moishe's Meats, which pretty much put it off my map since when I was seven I was unlikely to want to browse in a butcher's store that had slabs of dead cows and featherless chickens in its window as if that would really draw people in. I think that'd be true even if I weren't a vegetarian. Then it was The Nickel House, which sold newspapers and comics and other things that cost a lot more than a nickel. They went out of business, maybe because you can't lie in your store's name and expect to get away with it for long. And then someone named Herb bought it and I guess gave up on trying to figure out what he would be selling, so it became the This 'n That Store, which was exactly what it was. But, throughout all this time, the old Pick-a-Chick sign stayed where it was, running the long way up the side of the brick building. By the time it got to Herb, the Pick-a-Chick sign was practically a local landmark. So, there the sign hung on the This 'n That store although chicken was one of the few things you absolutely couldn't get there.

My parents hadn't exactly outlawed Herb's, but they weren't crazy about my going there since there was hardly anything in there that was Good For Me. Candy but no fruit. Comics but no books. Joke soap that turns your hands black but no ruled notebook paper. So, when I went, I tried to do it on the way to somewhere else so I could just sort of sidle on in.

Sidling is the right word because Herb – whoever he was – had put in three rows of shelves where only two really fit. So you had to walk sideways, and if you ran into someone in the same aisle, one of you had to back up all the way and move down another aisle. In fact, I always thought it cruel that Herb put the diet foods in the middle of one of the aisles, because if you really needed them, you probably wouldn't be able to fit in to get them.

But that's not why I was there on that Monday. My violin lesson was over and I thought I would treat myself to a Ding Dong Doggie before walking the eight blocks back home. You know you have to really like Ding Dong Doggies to be willing to ask for one by name. What Ding and Dong and Doggie had to do with a butterscotch cake with vanilla creme insides I'll never know. But I liked them, and so I sidled on in to the Pick-a-Chick.

I had my Ding Dong Doggie – please, can I just call it a "triple D" from now on? – I had my Triple D in my hand and headed to the counter to pay for it. But there was a woman ahead of me buying lottery tickets. She had filled out 20 forms where you choose what number you want to bet on, and Mrs. Karchov was typing the numbers into the lottery machine on the counter. One by one. At that rate, before I got home I'd be old enough to shave.

So, I dug my hand into my pocket and fished for coins. But a Triple D costs 85 cents – and is worth every penny – and who ever has 85 cents in coins? If I did I could have just left them on the counter and showed the Triple D to Mrs. Karchov. It's the type of cutting ahead in line that you're allowed to do, at least according to my father who sometimes pays for newspapers that way. But, since I didn't have the coins, all I could do is leave the dollar bill I had clutched in my hand. And I'd be darned if I was going to pay an extra fifteen cents for a Triple D. Money doesn't grow on trees you know. (By the way, neither do anvils. And it's a good thing.)

So, I waited. And waited. And Mrs. Karchov typed and typed. And I watched the lady in front of me. She was older than my mother but not as old as my grandmother. Somewhere in between. But nothing else was in-between about her. She was built like the original Starship Enterprise: not very high, very wide, and, because of her hat, flat on top. Without her hat, she wouldn't have looked very much like a starship at all. The hat was round like a pancake with a double pat of butter on top. It was blue, like the color of fake blueberry syrup. It looked like it was made out of some sort of shiny plastic that was sticky the way your fingers are when you're done with your pancakes. In fact, the whole thing looked like maybe she'd gotten it at the International House of Bad Hats.

And the woman seemed a bit nervous or unsure of herself. She kept muttering apologies and politenesses like, "Here's another, if you don't mind," and "I'm sorry to be such a bother," and "I do appreciate all your help." And after about every third ticket was typed in, she'd turn to me and half smile to let me know she felt bad about holding me up.

The thing was that she didn't have to make Mrs. Karchov do all that typing. The lottery machine in the store is a computer and it's perfectly happy to choose numbers for you. There's no reason to pick your own numbers, unless you think that you have some type of direct connection to the bouncing balls they use to pick the winning numbers every week. The only thing picking your own numbers does is make Mrs. Karchov stand there and type them in.

I know about this because my dad is the type of parent who doesn't just tell you not to do something but has to explain to you every detail of what it is that you're not supposed to do. For example, when he told me not to pour paint remover down the sink after washing out the brushes I'd used to decorate a model car, he didn't just tell me not to, he also told me everything human beings have learned about the effect of flammable solutions on the environment.

And when he told me not to play the lottery, I also learned everything known to science about it. Oh, this was a rich topic for Dad. It took most of the trip to overnight camp – a three hour drive – for me to find out exactly how lotteries work, their effect on the economy, their history throughout the ages, and why they are evil. As a result, I knew more about the lottery than I learned about U.S. history in an entire year of seventh grade. (No offense, Mr. Saperstein!)

Too bad the woman ahead of me didn't know what I knew. If she did, she wouldn't be playing the lottery at all, or else she'd have just let the machine pick her numbers for her. And my entire amazing experience wouldn't have happened.

Or if I'd just been willing to give up the fifteen cents, I would have slapped the dollar on the counter and been on my semi-merry way.

But no, I waited while Mrs. Karchov typed and the woman ahead of me kept looking at me apologetically. And finally, the woman was done. Almost. She paid for her lottery tickets with a crisp twenty dollar bill. And, then, at the last minute, when I thought my turn had finally come, she remembered she had also bought a bag of buttons. She pulled it out of the pocket of her orange jacket, and said, "Oh my! I almost walked out of here without paying for these!" Another two dollars changed hands, and at long last the woman was done. Nothing stood between me and my Triple D except handing Mrs. Karchov my dollar bill and getting my change back.

I placed the bill on the counter and heard the sound of about a hundred little taps. Without even looking I knew the lady had dropped the bag of buttons. "Oh my!" she said.

The floor was polka-dotted with buttons. "Let me help," said I, for I happen to be a nice boy...you can ask anyone. The woman barely fit in the Pick-a-Chick at all, and there was no way she was going to be able to squat and pick up the buttons.

So, down I went on my knees, and gathered the buttons, at first several at a time, and then, as they became harder to find, one by one. And I did a good job. Some were obvious, but others had skittered under shelves like mice afraid of a cat. But I peered and bent and twisted and felt until I thought I had them all.

"Thank you so much," the woman said over and over again as I hunted down the buttons. And when I was done, she said, "You really are the kindest boy. Your parents must be very proud of you."

"Yes, ma'am," I said because it seemed like the sort of thing a kind boy would say, especially if his parents were very proud of him. In fact, I think it was probably the first and only time I ever called anyone "ma'am." The truth is, all I could think about was getting my Triple D and rushing on home before my parents started picking a photo for the "Have you seen ..." posters they'd be putting on the telephone poles.

"Here," she said, "you must take one of these as a reward," handing me the top lottery ticket in her pile.

"Oh, I couldn't," I said, thinking about the expression on my parents' faces if I came home not only late but with a lottery ticket in my hand.

"Oh, you really must," she said, handing it to me. And being a nice boy, and a kind boy, and a boy who really wanted to eat a Ding Ding Doggie, I said, "OK. Thank you very much." And, without thinking much about it, I opened my violin case a crack and shoved the ticket into it.

"And if you win," said the woman, "you can think of me as your fairy godmother."

"Thank you. Goodbye," I said, in a pretend cheerful voice. But what I was thinking was, "Yeah, and the day I win the lottery will be the same day I'll think that my sister Maddie is fun to be with and, oh yeah, pigs can fly."

It just shows you how wrong you can be.

Chapter 2

I didn't think about the ticket again until Tuesday night. After all, everyone knows that if you have a violin lesson on Monday, you don't have to practice until twenty-four hours later. Even parents understand this. It's practically a law.

So, of course, I didn't open my violin case until Tuesday night. I had just finished my math homework and figured I'd get my violin practicing over with. This turned out to be lucky for me for two reasons. First, it meant that I opened up my case in my room, instead of in the den where I usually practice, so that when the lottery ticket fluttered out, no one saw it but me. Second, having just finished working on math problems put me in the right frame of mind.

I had just been busting my brain on those problems where you have to figure out what the next number is by catching on to the pattern in the numbers before it. For example, if the series were 1,3,7,15 the next number would be 31 because between 1 and 3 is 2, and between 3 and 7 is 4, and between 7 and 15 is 8, so you keep multiplying the difference by two and adding it. And that turns out to be the same thing as multiplying by two and adding one. How almost interesting!

So, when the lottery ticket floated off of my violin and fluttered down to the floor, for the first time I saw the number that the hat lady had picked. 35-8-27-9-18-9. Now, normally I have a real hard time with these types of problems, but this one I got right away, even though there was no reason to think there was anything to get. Maybe that's why I got it. Or maybe it was just that I noticed that the digits of the first number – 35 – added up to the second number. And, then, while I was at it, I noticed that if you subtract the second number from the first one – 35 minus 8 – you get the third number. And, wouldn't you know it, if you add the digits of the third number, you get the fourth. And if you subtract the fourth from the third, you get the fifth. And if you add the digits of the fifth, you get the sixth.

Coincidence? Maybe. If you look hard enough at any series you can begin to find some ways they work out. But this was too neat. The woman in the Pick-a-Chick must have had her own twisted mathematical mind working overtime in picking her numbers.

But I had more important things to worry about: I had to finish my violin practicing in time to be able to watch *The Simpsons* rerun on TV. So, I put the ticket back in my violin case and got to work.

And there it stayed … until the next day.

I was in the den, playing Commander Keen on the kids' computer. Keen's an old game, but it's a real time waster and because there's no blood and gore, my parents practically encourage me to play it. My mother was sitting at the roll-top desk, going over the bills, opening envelopes and shaking her head. And in comes my sister Maddie, holding the ticket, and saying, "What's this?" all innocently.

Maddie, you have to understand, is five years old and enough to drive any brother insane. She's the worst variety of cute: the type that's cute and knows it. All she has to do is pull

11

her little lower lip under her upper one and look at her shoes and shuffle her feet, and you can practically hear a crowd say "Awww." And then she gets what she wants.

Not that there's anything really wrong with that. I'd do it too, if I could get away with it. But, Maddie seemed to me to be doing it more and more, as if recognizing that she was only about a birthday away from it not working for her anymore. You had to give her credit. She was milking it for all it was worth.

I was out of my seat in a flash, thinking about how to explain how I ended up with the ticket when, to my amazement, my mother actually ignored Maddie. The telephone rang, and Mom was annoyed enough about being interrupted while working on the bills that she went for the phone to stop it from ringing as if it were a chipmunk she had to chase out of the house. So, while Mom was on the phone with someone trying to sell her another credit card – I pity the poor slob on the other end of the line – I was in Maddie's face and had grabbed the ticket from her.

"But what is it?" she asked..

"I'll tell you later. Now just keep quiet or I'll tell Mom you were playing with my violin again." Quickly shoving the ticket into my pocket, I went back to Keen, Maddie wandered back to her room, and my mother hung up on the guy from the credit card company with an evil smirk on her face.

That night, Maddie came into my room to borrow my good markers. There was a reason why they were mine and not Maddie's. They were permanent. Real permanent. I'd scientifically proved this when I was five and decided that the living room couch would look much better with a picture of our dog on it. Eight years later our dog was gone, the couch was in the "recreation room" in the basement, and my lovely drawing was still there in all its original color. Permanently. (By the way, you may be able to figure out why we call the recreation room the "wreck" room for short.)

"No," I said to Maddie, "you know you're not supposed to use these markers."

"But I have to color in a picture for school tomorrow."

"So what's wrong with yours?"

"They stink," she whined. Normally I would have corrected her language, not because I really care about the word "stink" but because it's my obligation as an older brother to be as annoying as possible. But her markers really did stink. The yellow stank like old bananas, the brown like fake chocolate, the red like cherry-flavored cough medicine. Her markers *really* stank. Plus, they didn't draw very well.

"If you get a single dot on anything except the paper, I'm the one who'll be blamed. And I'll take it out on you," I promised. I got down the marker set and, holding it just out of her reach, added, "Want them?"

"Yes, I just said that." She grabbed for them but I was faster.

"Want them? Want them?" Oh, I was being a real jerk.

"I'll be careful" she pleaded, trying to jump up to reach the markers.

"I know you will. But when five-year-olds are careful, somehow the rug ends up with marker marks in it."

"Let me use them!"

"Nope. I'm not going to take the blame for when you make a mistake and write your name on the rug."

"Give me the markers."

"Or what? You'll bite my ankles?"

"Or I'll tell Mom and Dad that you bought a lottery ticket."

Well, that got a fast reaction from me. I pushed the markers further back on my highest shelf. "Definitely not," I said.

"OK, then I'm going to tell anyways."

I have to admit, Maddie knew how to fight. Of course, she learned everything she knew from me. That's the problem with being the oldest – all the brilliant techniques you invented are stolen by the ones who come after you. It's the price of being a pioneer.

So I thought for a moment. There was really only one way to absolutely force Maddie to keep the lottery ticket a secret. "Maddie," I said, "I'll tell you what. I'm going to give you a great deal. Bargain of a lifetime. Shut up about the ticket, and not only will I lend you my markers, but I'll let you share my ticket. Ninety-ten."

"What do you mean?"

The poor thing hadn't gotten to percentages yet in school. "That means that if I win, I'll give you ten cents out of every dollar that I win."

"You'll give me ten cents?" She seemed happy enough with the ten pennies, but I didn't feel like I could really cheat her that way.

"Not exactly. I'll give you ten cents for every dollar I win. So, if I win thirty dollars, I'll give you three dollars and I'll keep 27 dollars. And if I win a hundred dollars, I'll give you ten dollars and I'll keep ninety dollars."

"You're going to give me ten dollars?" This was just about beyond her comprehension.

"Yes, but only if the ticket wins a hundred dollars. Never mind, just believe me that it's a great deal."

"I'm going to get ten dollars!"

I'd created a monster. Somehow now she believed that not only was I lending her the markers, but I was going to fork over ten bucks. I gave it one last try: "But only if the lottery ticket wins. If it doesn't win, neither of us will get any dollars at all."

"Ten dollars!" she said, as I handed her the marker set. But I could tell that she understood. Now she was being the jerk.

But at least now she was my partner in crime and wouldn't go blabbing to our parents – not if it was going to cost her ten dollars.

So, confident that my secret was safe – because now it was *our* secret – I tucked the ticket back into my violin case and began practicing "A Sailor's Shanty" over and over and over again.

Chapter 3

Life at Horace J. Oakes Middle School is far more complex than most people realize. It's a school where popularity counts more than just about anything. You could be the captain of the hockey team, a straight A student, great looking, and the star of this year's play – *The Music Man,* in case you were wondering – but if word got out that you were unpopular, well, you might as well find a cave with cable TV because you're not going to be doing a lot else with your time.

Of course, if you were all those things, you'd probably be popular too. But that's the thing – it's only a probability. Popularity is one of those things that's hard to judge, like trying to decide if you're good looking by staring into a mirror. You just can't tell. You can tell if you're smart by looking at a report card (at least kind of), and you can tell if you're a good athlete by seeing how fast you run a race, but popularity is hard to measure.

And it's also a little bit like being a celebrity who's famous just for being famous. Once word gets out that you're popular, well then, you're popular. But if you're popular and no one knows it, then you're not really popular. You can't say, "I'm popular, although everyone disagrees," any more than you can say, "I'm famous, but no one knows it."

Mind if I change the subject? I'm beginning to get a headache …

Anyway, the truth is that I could not claim to be one of the most popular kids in school. It's not that if you were to divide the school into two teams, The Populars and the Unpopulars, I would be made the captain of the Unpops. In fact, you'd really have to make a third team, the Who Cares, and then I definitely would be on the starting line up.

It beats me why that is. I'm not the irritating sort of kid who tries to get people to notice him by hanging upside down on the jungle gym in the playground until the change drops out of his pockets and his face turns red, and his shirt has fallen so that his flabby belly is on display, and drool starts dribbling from his mouth, and he's yelling, "I'm Bat Boy! I'm Bat Boy!" No, that's not me. That's my best friend Ari.

I just get along with most everyone and am especially liked by just about no one.

But at the beginning of the school year, I figured out a way to fix all that. Since you're popular if people think you're popular, Ari and I decided to create a club for popular people. It was a very exclusive club. Invitation only – and secret. The only two known members were Ari and me.

We called it "The Scutters Society" because "Scutters" didn't mean anything but sounded kind of cool – sort of like the word "popular." The Scutters Society had a secret meeting place, secret meetings, secret activities, and secret members.

Of course there wasn't really any such thing.

But we started dropping hints about it. I printed up a notice of an upcoming meeting, and then crumpled it and left it in the hallway near a garbage can, hoping someone would notice it and read it. Not even Mr. Carbone did when he picked it up and threw it out.

I wrote up the minutes of a meeting and left it in a desk in study hall so that the next occupant would find it. The minutes referred to members by code names that I hoped would be obvious to anyone who read it. For example, Joel Hess (captain of the soccer team and immensely popular – and obnoxious) was "Jewel Heist" and Kathy Picatino (fluent in French, awesomely beautiful – and obnoxious) was "Café Pick-a-Time-o." Ok, so it wasn't so subtle, but the whole point was for the names to be understood.

Then I sent in an anonymous tip to Louellen Parness who writes a gossip column for the Oakes Observer, our school paper. "Pop Quiz: What is the secret Scutters Society all about?" she wrote. "And just how popular do you have to be to get in? Give yourself a B if you answer: Very. But give yourself an A if you didn't even have to ask."

This turned out to be just about as dumb as it sounds. No one noticed, or if they did, they didn't care. Popular kids don't have to have secret societies. And even if people had noticed, they wouldn't have associated me and Ari with it because, as I may have mentioned, we're not popular.

So, by this time of the year, I had not only lost interest in it, I was embarrassed about it. But not Ari. He wanted to have meetings and was talking about running for vice president.

This Thursday, though, he wasn't asking for a meeting. He had a different idea. He wanted to form a rock and roll band called – guess what? – The Scutters. And I had agreed to try it out.

You see, although I struggle along with the violin, I'm

actually an OK guitar player, without any lessons. My mother plays – she was in a rock band when she was in high school, which I cannot possibly picture – so it was easy for me to pick it up. If you never heard me play violin, you might almost think that I have some musical talent.

My father drove me to Ari's house for the first rehearsal of The Scutters because it would have been be a little hard to fit my guitar and amplifier in my bike basket. When I got there, Ari was already banging away at his drums in his garage, and Mimi was playing bass. The result some might call progressive jazz and others might call modern music. I'd call it just plain bad.

But that's ok. It was our first rehearsal and the guitar player – me – hadn't even plugged in yet.

Mimi was my oldest friend. In fact, she was such an old friend that "friend" isn't even the right word. Mimi and I were in the same playgroup when we were twelve months old. When my Mom had to run out to take Maddie to the emergency room to have a shell from a Captain Galactica Thermo Nuclear Ray Gun rocket extracted from her nose, she called Marcie, Mimi's mom, to watch over me. When Marcie had an extra ticket for the Ice-O-Rama traveling skating extravaganza, it was natural for her to offer to take me. In fact, at the beginning of second grade, my mother actually let Marcie take me and Mimi shopping for clothes. Now that's trust.

So, I didn't feel too bad when I laughed in her face when I saw her sitting on Ari's little brother's tricycle, dressed in pink shorts, red sneakers, and a purple tee shirt that said "Just Say Huh?" – the very picture of a rock 'n roll queen.

We didn't play too much music that first rehearsal. We spent most of the time doing the basics: tuning our instruments, trying to get Ari to play softer, and arguing over the name of our first album – Ari liked "Meet the Scutters," Mimi liked "The Scutters Second Album" and I personally preferred "The Scutters Cut One."

At the end of the rehearsal, Mimi brushed her bangs out of her eyes and said, "Well, that was sort of fun," and we all agreed. Actually, it sort of was.

And who knows? If the Scutters actually became a popular band, wouldn't the three members of the Scutters themselves have to become popular? Maybe The Scutters Society, in its own way, was going to put us into the world of the popular.

Or so it seemed the day before I won the lottery.

Chapter 4

Friday was press day for my father. He publishes the local newspaper that comes out once a week. For the longest time I thought he hated it because whenever he talked about it, he was complaining: The local businesses weren't advertising, the ones who advertised weren't paying, the local residents weren't subscribing, the reporters weren't reporting. One complaint after another, sometimes for an entire dinner or Sunday morning walk.

So, when I asked him a few years ago why he didn't quit, he looked shocked. "Quit?? Jake, I love *The Gaz*. I wouldn't do anything else!" (*The Gaz* was short for *The Melville Gazette*.) "Why would you ask such a thing?" When I told him that all I ever heard from him were complaints, you could see it sink in. After that, my father did a terrible job trying to be positive about *The Gaz* around me. It was cute.

Fridays are tense days for my dad because that's the day the paper actually gets printed. It means he has to go to the printing plant to oversee the production. But it's also the last chance to discover and fix any last minute problems – and to find out that you made mistakes that now you can't fix because the paper's been printed.

So, at dinner on Friday, when my mom asks how Dad's day was, it's not like the other days where you just expect a "Fine" that doesn't mean anything. On Friday, Dad's answer tells us what the mood of dinner and of the weekend will be like.

Tonight, we got "Well, it's done, anyway," which long years

of listening to my father have taught me means: "Rough day, but, in the end the newspaper turned out fine."

It seems that at the last minute, Dad had to drop an article from the front page because the town committee on recycling hadn't met, so there was nothing to report about. "So, I pulled my editorial about lotteries onto the front page. I don't like putting editorials on the front page, but it was the only thing that would fit." (It's always surprising to me to find out that what goes on the front page of a newspaper can depend on things like what article is the right length instead of purely on what's most important. Another illusion shattered.)

"This is the last in the series, isn't it?" my mother asked as my Dad served her oven roasted potatoes.

"Yup. Which makes more sense than putting one in the middle of the series on the front page. In this last one, I summarize all the others."

I suddenly lost interest in the potatoes, normally one of my favorite foods. The front page announcement that my father hates the lottery while I had a lottery ticket ticking upstairs was making me uncomfortable.

I'd read Dad's editorials on the topic. My Dad is a good writer, I'll give him that. And I can't say I really disagreed with him. Here are his reasons:

First, the lottery was created to take the money poor people were spending on illegal gambling – a daily game called "the numbers" – and have that money come to the state government instead of to organized crime. So, the lottery started out as a way for the government to act like criminals.

Second, the lottery is a fool's game. The odds against winning are so large that if you bet every day of your life, your chances of coming out ahead in the end were about the same as the chance that you'd be hit by a pink car driven by a clown named Moe. You'd be far better off putting the same amount of money into a bank every day.

Third, the lottery is played more by poor people than by rich people, yet the money the state makes is spread evenly across all the towns. That means poor towns end up with less money than they started with. My Dad calls this a "tax on the poor."

Fourth, it encourages people to gamble. All the lottery advertisements make gambling sound like fun and a way to get rich quick.

Fifth, it's an inappropriate way to pay for educational programs (which is where the money the state makes goes). Educational programs shouldn't have to depend on people gambling.

My father wasn't a fanatic about this. He actually was reasonable on the topic. He just didn't always act that way. Once you got him started, he could go on for hours. His face would redden, his eyebrows would tie themselves in a knot, and he'd lean into whoever he was talking with as if he were just waiting for a chance to tell him why they were all wrong.

I don't think there was any other topic my father felt this way about.

Which is why the editorial ended up on the front page.

The first two parts of the series he'd been writing had

gotten a lot of people to send in letters, mainly disagreeing with him. Being a fair person, he had printed them all in the Letters to the Editor section – except one that began "Dear Jerk-faced Weasel."

"You know what the lottery is worth this week?" my father asked with just a little bitterness. "Over 100 million dollars. A hundred million dollars! Can you believe it? When I drove home, I saw a line coming out of the Pick-a-Chick store. People lining up to buy their tickets, last minute. Poor suckers. They might as well just put their dollar bills into the trash can in front of the store and skip the line."

I didn't ask him if he saw a woman there who looked like the Starship Enterprise. And I decided right after supper to make sure that my ticket was still safely hidden in my violin case.

So, we made it through dinner, and I practiced violin (and checked on my ticket), and then spent an hour working on some songs for The Scutters. In other words, it was turning into a normal Friday night.

The normal Friday routine is that I'm allowed to stay up until eleven to watch my favorite program, a medical detective show – although, the truth is that I wouldn't like the program nearly so much if it didn't give me an excuse to stay up until eleven. Then I go off to bed and my parents watch the local news on channel 5.

Between my show and the start of the news, channel 5 televises the drawing of the state lottery.

Having stayed up through the credits of my show, on

the grounds that the credits are legally a part of the show, we were still engaged in the standard good night chit chat when the sparkly toothed Ginny Wombach came on screen to announce the winner. Behind her was a machine that jumbled 40 numbered ping pong balls as if they were stuck in a berserk popcorn popper.

"Well, you'd better be turning in, Jake," said my father as the first number jumped out of the tumbler and was announced by the ever-smiling Ginny. It was 35. So far so good! But, I realized the odds of the next one being an eight – my next number – were 39 to one. There were 39 ways the wrong number could come up, and just one way the right one could. And that'd be true for the next five numbers. The odds were ridiculously bad.

But getting that first one right sure got my attention! So I stalled a bit, while pretending to pay no attention to the television. "Yeah," I said, "I'm pretty tired." Then a nice long yawn.

Ginny said, "And the next number is 8!" as if eight were an especially exciting number.

It was to me. 35-8-27-9-18-9. Those were the magic numbers. They were burned in my brain because of the sequence I had discovered within them.

"You know," I said, trying to keep my parents distracted from the TV, "tonight's episode was sort of disappointing. Predictable plot."

"Isn't it predictable every week?" Mom said. "Bad guys do something wrong, good guys catch them."

"Well, yes," I said as Ginny said "27!" I tried not to show that I was paying any attention to what Ginny was saying, but all I could think of was the next number: 9, 9, 9, 9! I continued, "But usually you can't figure out how they're going to catch them."

"That's true," said my father. "You could say the same thing about every mystery novel ever written. Bad guy murders someone, detective figures out who." My mother loves mystery novels.

This might have been fascinating conversation, but all I heard was Ginny saying, "And the next number is 9!" I was just two numbers away from winning!

At this point I was too distracted to be able to participate in the conversation and I just hoped the discussion I'd started would be carried on by Mom and Dad without me. I was looking at them, but my ears heard nothing but Ginny. Ginny was suddenly my favorite person in the whole world.

And she said my favorite word in the whole world: "Eighteen!" she squealed. It was all I could do not to squeal along with her. One number away.

Oh my gosh, I thought. Suppose I actually win. A hundred million dollars! But I wasn't thinking about what I could do with the money. I was thinking about how I'd ever tell my parents about it.

Still, there was one number to go. One chance in 36 that I'd win.

That's the moment my mother noticed that the lottery was on TV, and that's the moment she turned it off, saying, "What are we doing with this on!" I don't know if she noticed that I was paying attention to Ginny, or whether the conversation about how predictable mystery novels are just got too boring. But just as the ball popped out of the lottery basket and Ginny inhaled to burble the exciting last number ... Click!

"Ok, Jake, time for bed," said my father.

"You've been up late enough already," said my mother.

"Um, ok, I guess I'll be going to bed," I said, as if I weren't one number away from a hundred million dollars.

So I went to bed.

But not to sleep.

Chapter 5

The next morning I was not up bright and early.

That's because I was up dim and late the night before. I tossed. I turned. I practically did land-based synchronized swimming. My blankets were twisted around me as tightly as if elves had spent the evening practicing for their knot-tying merit badge. And when dawn finally came, I drifted off to sleep.

To sleep, and to dream. To dream about coming home from school with dollar bills stuffed into every pocket and down my shirt and in my cap and in my lunch box. Dollar bills hanging out all over me. And my mother and father were waiting for me, asking me how my school day had been and if I'd like a snack, while I frantically kept shoving bills back into their hiding places, hoping my parents wouldn't see.

It was nine thirty when I woke up, which was late for me on a Saturday morning. Even before breakfast, I made an excuse about getting some exercise, and hopped on my bike.

The Pick-a-Chick was open. Outside was a stack of newspapers. I grabbed one and raced inside, pulling a dollar from my pants pocket. Mrs. Karchov was feeling particularly chatty that day, and it seemed forever before she gave me my fifty cents change.

Thanking her – remember, I am a nice boy – I went outside, sat on the curb, and with trembling fingers looked up in the index where the winning lottery number was. Page 56. It's amazing how hard it can be to find a page when you really want to.

I knew I had five of the six numbers right. So, when I got to page 56, I read backwards, from right to left. There it was, in big beautiful black ink: 9.

I had won.

The prize, the paper said, was $111,000,000.

Now what was I going to do?

So I did what any red-blooded American boy would do: I stood up, made a fist, pulled my elbow in, and said, "Yes!"

That was the moment Ms. Floyd, my math teacher, decided to pass by.

"Why so excited?" she asked.

"Oh, um, my favorite team just won." This was desperate. I don't even have a favorite team. I have to keep reminding myself that baseball is the one with bases.

"Well, congratulations," she said, as she went into the Pick-a-Chick. I hate seeing teachers outside of school. It's so confusing.

I sat on the curb again, this time because I was beginning to feel dizzy thinking about what had just happened to me.

I had won $111,000,000.

I began to think of all the things I could buy. And after each thought popped in my head, there was a picture of my parents grounding me for 111,000,000 days.

A super CD player. Mom shaking her head.

A speed boat for our vacations on Lake Winpucket. Dad looking disappointed in me.

Brand new cars for my parents. Mom and Dad giving the keys back to the car salesperson.

Could I not accept the prize? Just pretend I had lost the ticket or the woman had never given it to me? But how can you turn down $111,000,000? I could give it all to charity, but I'm not that nice a boy.

I guess I wasn't looking so happy by the time the woman who looked like the Starship Enterprise came back out of the store, with new lottery tickets in her hand.

"Oh, hello!" she said cheerily.

"Hello," I said, avoiding her eyes.

"Oh dear, you seem upset?" she asked. "Can I help you?"

I practically laughed. "Not exactly," I said.

"What's bothering you?"

"Well," I said, "it's actually sort of your fault."

"My fault," the woman said in great surprise, putting her hand to her chest as if her heart were failing her.

"Only sort of." Now I had to explain. "Remember, you gave me that lottery ticket a couple of days ago because I helped you pick up some buttons that had spilled?"

"Yes, indeed. You were very kind."

"Just being polite."

"Well, it's nice to meet a young person who's learned his manners. The ticket was the least I could do for you."

"Was it worth $111,000,000 to you to have me help?"

"$111,000,000 …?"

"Yeah. The ticket you gave me won."

"No! Really?"

"Yup."

"Are you sure?"

"Totally. Do you know that your numbers were in a series?"

"Of course. It helps me pick numbers to use a little sequence like that. Otherwise, I spend forever trying to decide which numbers to pick. So you won?"

"Well, actually, you won," I said. "It was your ticket."

"Now, now. None of that. I gave it to you fair and square."

"But it doesn't seem right …"

"I wanted you to have it. But, oh, my, what are you going to do with all that money?"

"I have no idea."

"Is that's what's making you unhappy?" she asked kindly.

"Not really. My parents are dead set against playing the lottery."

"Oh, I see."

"In fact, my father has an editorial against it on the front page of this paper."

The woman unfolded a newspaper from under her arm. It was *The Gaz.* "You mean this article? This is your father? He's a

31

very good writer. The editorial makes a lot of sense." She was holding her lottery tickets in her other hand.

"So, I can't really tell them that I won."

"Well," she said, "Why don't come with me to the Soda Squirt and we'll sit down and try to figure this out?"

So we trudged across the street to the little green and white snack bar. "By the way," she said, "I'm Mrs. Fordgythe. Mrs. Moira Fordgythe. What's your name?"

"Jake," I said.

"Well, Jake, let's take a booth and have a soda," she said, seating herself at a red leather booth that barely held her.

"I'll pay," I said. "Um, actually," I said, checking my pockets, "you'll have to lend me some money …"

"Pshaw," she said, "Don't you worry about that."

The waitress came and I ordered a Coke, although I actually was in the mood for a Coke with a scoop of Cookies and Cream ice cream, which gets most of your dessert food groups into a single glass. Mrs. Fordgythe ordered "a simple glass of bubbly bottled water," – she patted her starship-like stomach – "And, oh, a slice of that dreamy looking cheese cake. And instead of a lime in my bubbly water, would you mind adding just a couple of squeezes of chocolate syrup and about two ounces of fresh cream? That would be so lovely, thank you, dear. Oh, and a scoop of pistachio ice cream on that cheese cake would be divine. Thank you so much."

We sat in the silence of two people who don't know each other sharing a booth at an ice cream shop.

"This must be very hard on you, poor dear," she said at last.

I nodded.

"Your parents must be very much against the lottery."

I nodded again.

"And they must have a lot of respect for you to think that you'd act on principle and not play the lottery."

I had to nod again. It was true, but I hadn't thought of it that way before.

"Well," she said, "I think I have an idea about how to get you your money without your parents knowing."

"You do?"

"Yes, but of course that isn't your problem."

"It's not?"

"No. Your real problem is getting your parents to understand how you came by a lottery ticket and why you should be allowed to keep your winnings."

That was true, too.

"What's your plan for getting me the money?"

"Oh, it's a very good plan, I think. Trust me."

I didn't say anything. To trust someone, you should know them well enough to think that there aren't any odd quirks that may make them act in ways you couldn't predict. And so far Mrs. Fordgythe was all quirks. But I did trust her. I couldn't tell you why.

"What do I have to do?" I asked.

"You have to lend me your ticket for a few days."

"But why can't you just come explain to my parents that you gave me the ticket because I helped you out?"

"Oh, no no no," she said, "I don't think that would be wise at all. You parents will think that you shouldn't have accepted the ticket, and I would so much like to help you find a way to keep the money."

Just then our food arrived and seemed to wipe all thought of lottery tickets, parents and 111 million dollars out of Mrs. Fordgythe's mind. All that existed for her was her spoon, her mouth, and Mount Dessert.

When she was done, with a satisfied smile on her lips, she said, "Ahh. That was refreshing."

And I handed her my lottery ticket, slightly bent from its trip in my pocket.

"What are you going to do with it?" I asked, which really meant, "Am I ever going to see it – or you – again?"

"Thank you, Jake," she said as she took it. "I really think this plan will work."

"How will I know?"

"Come back to the Pick-a-Chick on Wednesday around 3. Is that all right?"

"But suppose you have to reach me before that?"

"I can always give you a call."

"But you don't know my number."

"Don't be silly. 'Richter' is in the phone book."

The waitress came back and left the bill on our table. I stuck my hand in my pocket, looking for money, but then remembered that I only had the fifty cents change from the newspaper. I looked at Mrs. Fordgythe, embarrassed. "Oh don't be silly, dear," she said, as she left money for the bill. "You don't have your hundred and eleven million dollars yet!"

We stood up to go. I felt much lighter without the ticket in my pocket. Mrs. Fordgythe touched me on the arm and said, "I'll see you on Wednesday, dear. Now don't you worry about a thing."

For a moment I didn't. And then I had a sudden thought. "Wait, Mrs. Fordgythe," I called to her back as she began to walk away. "I have a question."

"Yes, dear," she said sweetly, turning towards me.

"I never told you my last name. How did you know it?" I could almost hear the dramatic background music as the detective uncovers the clue that gives it all away.

She pointed to her copy of the *Gaz*. "It says your father's name right here, dear."

"Oh, yeah. That's right."

"Don't worry about a thing," she said to me again and left.

Chapter 6

"Easy come, easy go," is what I told myself all the way home. It's not like I ever really had the money, so I couldn't really lose it. Still, my pockets felt mighty empty walking home.

But, whatever feelings I had that I might have made a mistake were erased as I stepped in the door. "Shhh," my mother insisted, "your father's on TV."

Sure enough, there was Dad being interviewed on a local news program. "It doesn't matter, Connie," he was saying to the host of the program, "the lottery is nothing but gambling – backed and encouraged by your tax dollars."

The woman seated next to him started to talk, but Dad went right on. "You know what really bothers me? The fact that our government runs advertisements encouraging people to gamble."

The woman spoke up. "Still, I'd rather have the government run the lottery and have the money go to education than have organized crime run it and have the money go to them."

"Oh, Laureen," my father said, "You might as well say that the government ought to start selling cocaine because it's better than having criminals do it. And then you'd see advertisements telling you how great cocaine is! That's exactly the situation we're in with the lottery."

The host jumped in to point out that the lottery wasn't exactly the same as selling drugs, but my father was just gathering steam. Knowing that the lottery ticket was out of my hands made it a lot easier for me to watch the rest of the program.

That afternoon, when my father came home – still with a patch of makeup from the TV appearance on his forehead – we all told him what a great job he had done.

"The producers of the show thought I did pretty well, too," he said, obviously quite pleased about something. "In fact," he added, pausing to keep us in suspense, "they want me to create a special debate on the topic 'Lottery: Yes or No.' And I'd be the spokesperson for the No side."

"That's wonderful," said my mother.

"What's a 'nose hide'?" my sister asked.

"What's a nose hide?" I asked, completely confused. "Boogers?"

"No, no" my mother said, "Maddie wants to know what a 'No side' is. It's someone who disagrees with something. He's on the side that says No. That's all."

I liked my answer better.

"Can I be on the TV show?" asked Maddie.

Dad and Mom laughed. "Maybe when you're older. It's really for grownups."

"But that's not all," my father said. "If it goes well, they think they'd like me to host a whole series!"

"My daddy the TT star!" said Maddie. We all laughed because "TT" had been my old nanny's cute way of saying "TV."

Maddie hadn't ever met her, but Aunt Flo (as we called her) lived on in family legend, along with one of my grandfather's old hat customers who used to recite the poem "Hiawatha" to me whenever I saw him. And there was my father's childhood dog Whiskers who once ate an entire plate of brownies off the kitchen table and then knocked over a glass of milk and drank it. I suppose every family has a set of characters that somehow get turned into legends like this.

With my father becoming more and more famous for his anti-lottery stand, the fact that I'd probably never see that lottery ticket again should have been a relief. But I lay in bed unable to sleep for over an hour that night, thinking about what I could have done with a hundred and eleven million dollars. I mainly thought of really dumb things like buying a yacht and completely filling it with those plastic egg-like containers you get from the quarter vending machines. Would $111,000,000 – 440 million of the containers – be enough? It's really hard to figure. Besides, if it took ten seconds to put a quarter in and turn the handle, it would take 1,222,222 hours just to get them all. That's over 50,000 days. That's over 139 years. I fell asleep as I was figuring in Leap Years. Then I woke up in the middle of the night and thought about buying a collection of the world's best electric guitars, with every musical gadget ever invented. I tried listing them to put myself to sleep, and had gotten up to treble boosting wah-wah's with bass thumper reverb, when I finally dropped off.

I woke up feeling like I had lost something. Only after shaking my head a couple of times did I realize that I was feeling the loss of the hundred and eleven million dollars I never actually had.

On Mondays, I usually feel rich because I have my five dollars of allowance in my pocket. But this Monday I felt poor because what's $5 compared to the one hundred and eleven million dollars I didn't have?

Our gym teacher let us out ten minutes early, and I hooked up with Ari outside, watching some of the older kids shoot hoops. We could have tried to join, but seeing them sigh and roll their eyes made it not worth even asking. So we just sat on our heels and talked. Ari told me about a really annoying visit to his uncle during which his father and uncle almost got into a fistfight over a stupid ping pong game. When he was done, he said, "So, what did you do this weekend?"

I almost replied, "Won a hundred and eleven million dollars. And then gave it to this lady who looks like a starship." But there seemed no point. More important, I discovered that a part of me was still thinking that Mrs. Fordgythe might actually show up with the money.

People are funny, aren't we? Or maybe not funny so much as just complicated. Here I was feeling poor because I was convinced I never was going to see the lottery money again, but another part of me was saying, "Now, don't be too hasty. You may get the money after all."

I can't figure me out. How can anyone expect me to figure out other people?

Especially Ari. Monday night we had another rehearsal of our band. When I got there, you didn't have to be a member of the Psychic Friends Network to know that something was bothering Ari. He was sitting on an old coffee table that had been in his garage forever, studying his shoelaces, and barely lifted his head to say hello. Mimi was reading an old copy of *People* magazine.

"Hey, Ari," I said. "What's bothering you?"

"Nothing."

This is all part of the ritual we all seem to go through. Boys, anyway. When someone asks what's bothering you, you always have to deny that anything is wrong at least three times before you can admit it. Ari, being Ari, however, didn't quite play along. I only had to ask him one more time.

I wasn't prepared for what he had to say, though. I expected something like: "I just realized that Wiley Coyote isn't ever going to catch the Roadrunner," or "My parents won't let me paint my room black," or even "I think my athlete's foot has spread to my liver."

I was not ready for: "I'm in love."

As a little tiny chuckle escaped me – I really should get credit for not laughing out loud right in his face – it struck me that I wasn't being fair. What was wrong with Ari falling in love? Sure, he acted odd, and had strange ways of expressing himself, but he had feelings like anyone else. And, more to the point, he was allowed to make as big a jerk out of himself as anyone else. I'm not saying that everyone who falls in love is a jerk. Some people become jerks once they fall in love. That's been my experience so far, anyway. ("Wait until it happens to you," is what my twenty-year-old cousin Melinda says, and she's not a jerk.)

"In love?" I said. "I thought that was supposed to make you happy."

"Me too. But only if she loves you back."

"Who?"

"Amanda."

"Amanda Dunn?" Mimi and I both asked at the same time. This wasn't funny. This was bizarre. And maybe even dangerous.

Ari just looked at his sneakers and nodded to them glumly.

"Amanda Dunn," I said again. Amanda Dunn-it as she was known because if you named something you'd always wanted to do, Amanda had done it. Wind surfing, backstage pass to a top concert, a first class flight to Bermuda to go scuba diving with a private tutor, have your own credit card...Amanda's Done It. Her parents owned the Dunn Regency, Dunn Manufacturing, the Dunn Towers, Dunn Estates and Dunn Village – an apartment building, an office building, a community of houses, and an apartment block mainly occupied by old people. All had the name "Dunn" written on them in the same ugly cursive script taller than Stretch Levine, our star basketball player. My father had published a couple of articles about Dunn Village because some people claimed that Mr. Dunn was letting the place get run down so that the old people there would leave and the Dunns could rent the apartments to people with more money. There was no hard proof, but I believed it anyway.

Amanda's life seemed to revolve around the fact that her family was rich. There were the big things like the fact that she was always perfectly dressed and looked down on anyone she thought wasn't her equal. And there were the little things like the fact that she started every day with a new ballpoint pen, not even trying to use up the old one.

Ari and Amanda? Hard to imagine.

And it was just as hard to imagine what Ari saw in Amanda. Ari didn't care about clothes. That was obvious from how he dressed. He didn't care about money, so long as he had enough to buy a triple shake at the Soda Squirt. Ari didn't even care about girls – at least until now.

So, after pretending to be suddenly fascinated by an oil can on the window of Ari's garage so that I could keep my head turned away from him as I put on a proper expression, I said calmly, "Oh really? When did this start?"

Ari sat on his amplifier, his skinny legs swinging in his very wide shorts. "Forever," he said in a dreamy sort of voice as if he was talking not to me but to the clouds. "Or yesterday."

"What happened?"

"Well, I was skateboarding home." That would explain the scabs on his knees, elbows and hands, and the scratches on his cheek, arms and ankle – Mrs. Rumple's sticker bush always seemed to catch him. "And there she was, walking with Lydia Marmon. We were on Hillside Hill, so we were going about the same speed. So I could hear her talking." He said "her" as if he he was not worthy of saying her name. His eyes were wet and melty.

After watching this longer than I wanted to, I prodded him. "And what was she saying?"

"It was like bells. Little silvery bells."

"And what was she talking about?"

"About the dance. Ah, the dance …" Ari drifted off, probably thinking about whisking her around the dance floor in a swirl of glitter.

"What about the dance?"

"She can't go," he said.

"Why not?"

"Her father's grounded her. The rogue!" His face was turning red with anger. I don't think I'd ever heard anyone use the term "rogue" before.

"What happened?"

"She lost her father's Terwilliger Spoon."

"His what?"

"Terwilliger Spoon. I'm pretty sure that's what she said. Her voice was so silvery…."

Before he could get lost in the memory of her tinkling voice, I sharpened my tone and asked, "Do you know what that is?"

"I think it was something that was passed down in his family. Mr. Dunn collects spoons. She said something like, 'At least I didn't borrow one of the spoons with jewels in it,' so I guess some have diamonds and rubies in them."

"Why did she borrow it?"

"For a little tea party she was giving. Maybe someday she'll invite me to one ..."

As far as I knew, Ari wouldn't know which end of a teapot to pour from. Love does strange things to people.

Suddenly, it was as if Ari heard how dopey he sounded. He blushed. "Let's practice," he insisted, and he wouldn't let us stop for two hours.

Have I mentioned that love does strange things to people?

Chapter 7

Wednesday came as slowly as a slug moving across an open-faced peanut butter and jelly sandwich. (You don't want to know how I know about that.)

Wednesday was the day when Mrs. Fordgythe was supposed to tell me how she was going to get me my lottery winnings. Or, as I thought, Wednesday was the day when I would know for sure that Mrs. Fordgythe had done what any normal person would have done: cashed in my lottery ticket and moved to Disneyland.

I was coming home from school when Mrs. Fordgythe suddenly was next to me. I didn't see her coming, but somehow she had glided into place and was saying my name, asking me to walk more slowly.

"Mrs. Fordgythe!" I said in surprise, almost shock.

"Good day," she said.

For a moment I almost expected her to start to gloat: "I have a hundred and eleven million dollars and you don't."

But instead she said, "I have splendid news!"

"What is it?"

"I've found a way to give you your money without anyone knowing about it. Well, hardly anyone."

"How?" I asked.

"Come with me," she replied, taking me by the elbow and steering me towards the center of town.

Ahead of us was the First Dominion Trust. Some of the newer banks in town looked like motels or drive-through fast food joints. But not the old First Dominion. It was made of gray concrete and marble, with front doors so large that you could fit an elephant through them, which would be useful because it probably took an elephant to pull the doors closed every night. As Mrs. Fordgythe and I mounted the steps, I could feel the warm smell of the bank – like the scent of a desk drawer you haven't opened in a couple of years – wrap around me.

Our steps echoed behind us all the way inside until we reached a wooden desk with a sign that said "Julia Minder." Ms. Minder looked up and seemed pleased. "Mrs. Fordgythe! We've been looking forward to your visit. I'll go get Ms. Harrigan."

In all my years of coming to the First Dominion – usually accompanying my mother on an errand – I had never made it to a desk, only to the counter where tellers stand behind bars and count out cash. Now Ms. Minder was taking us beyond the desks, all the way to a private office. She knocked on the door and swung it open. As soon as she saw us, Ms. Harrigan was on her feet and coming towards us, with her right hand in front of her, ready for a shake.

"Come in, come in," said Ms. Harrigan. "Mrs. Fordgythe, Mrs. Fordgythe! This must be Jacob Richter." She shook both our hands. She was older than my mother but younger than Mrs. Fordgythe, and was dressed in a gray skirt with a gray jacket and some type of white scarf that entirely covered her neck and almost reached past her chin. "Have a seat, have a seat." Apparently she was the type of person who likes to say things twice just to convince you she meant it the first time. She

46

had us sit in the red leather chairs in front of her desk.

We were apparently very popular at this bank.

"Well, well," said Ms. Harrigan. "So this is our new depositor."

"Actually," said Mrs. Fordgythe, "he's not a new depositor at all."

"No, not at all, not at all," said Ms. Harrigan, "But he's about to become our largest."

"What do you mean?" I asked. I didn't want to admit that I knew what was going on until I knew it for a fact.

Ms. Harrigan smiled and said "Mrs. Fordgythe is about to make a little gift to you, a little gift." She nodded to Mrs. Fordgythe who rummaged in her enormous pocket book for what seemed like three days.

"Oh my, where is it? I know I had it this morning," she said as we listened to the rustlings and clankings of her bag as she fished around. I practically expected her to dive headfirst into it and emerge wearing scuba gear. "Oh, yes, here it is," she said at last, holding a light blue rectangular piece of paper in her hand.

She gave it to me.

I looked at it. It was a check. It was made out to me.

The amount was $110,999,997.46.

My hand began to shake so I rested it on the desk.

"For me?" I finally said.

Mrs. Fordgythe nodded.

I must have been in shock because the first thing I thought of wasn't what I could do with so much money. It was instead why it wasn't an even $111,000,000. It's not that I cared about the missing couple of dollars. I was just curious. But I didn't want to look like the stingiest person in history by asking.

Instead, I dug deep inside my soul to find the exact words to express my feelings. I think I came up with something pretty poetic. "Holy cow!" I said.

"Holy cow, holy cow," repeated Ms. Harrigan. She seemed like a nice woman, but I was suddenly glad she wasn't my mother. It would have driven me nuts, driven me nuts.

She continued, "Mrs. Fordgythe used your lottery ticket to pick up the money from the Lottery Commission, and then came here to make sure that we could put it into your account without having to tell anyone else. Which, of course, we can do."

"Holy cow," I said again, brilliantly.

"Yes, it was quite a little adventure going to the Lottery Commission," said Mrs. Fordgythe. "They were very nice about it. They didn't seem very excited, but I suppose giving out millions of dollars becomes just part of a day's work after a while."

"Aren't you going to be in the newspapers because you won?"

"No. They passed a law a few months ago. Winners were getting so pestered by people asking for money that the lottery officials aren't allowed to give out the name of the winner, unless the winner wants."

"Even if the winner is a kid?"

"Well, I don't know about that. But officially, a kid didn't win it. An old lady did."

"Aw, you're not so old, Mrs. Fordgythe."

"That's very polite of you, Jake, but I know exactly how old I am, and I'm an old lady. In any case, let's get this check deposited to your account."

Ms. Harrigan leaned over and pointed to the back of the check. "Just sign your name here, here."

I took the pen Ms. Harrigan offered. I was so nervous that I made the "J" in "Jake" especially large and wondered if that would mean the check wouldn't count. But Ms. Harrigan didn't seem to care. She took the check back from me, held it up admiringly, and said, "Very good, very good. Congratulations, Jake, we'll put this in your account as of this afternoon, this very afternoon."

"Great," I said. "But there's something else I have to do."

"You'd like to withdraw some money? No problem, no problem."

"Yes, please."

"How much?" asked Ms. Harrigan.

"Eleven million dollars, please."

This took the wind out of Ms. Harrigan's sails. "Eleven, um, eleven, um, eleven, um..."

"I promised to split the winnings with my sister. Ten percent. She has an account here, too."

"Then it shouldn't be any problem at all, at all."

"Very good of you to keep your promise, Jake," said Mrs. Fordgythe.

I didn't know what to say because it hadn't occurred to me that I might not keep my promise: the curse of being a nice boy.

"So," said Ms. Harrigan, "Would you like to withdraw a little pocket money for you to have to spend? Might be useful, be useful."

"Well, sure, I guess."

"How much?"

"I don't know. How about ten dollars?"

Mrs. Fordgythe responded, "Well, Jake, you don't want to have to keep coming back to the bank. It might make people suspicious. I think you ought to withdraw a little more than that."

"Fifteen?" Mrs. Fordgythe shook her head. "Twenty? Fifty? A hundred dollars??!" Mrs. Fordgythe finally nodded. "A hundred dollars seems like an awful lot."

Ms. Harrigan smiled. "Jake, we're going to invest your money so that you're going to be earning ten percent on your 100 million dollars. That means that if you don't spend any of it, in a year, the 100 million dollars in your bank account will earn ten million dollars. Just by not spending it. And later we need to talk about ways to invest the money so you can make more than that. I really think we'd need to have your parents involved in any discussion of investments." Mrs. Fordgythe nodded.

"But my parents don't have to know about this, right?"

"Absolutely not. I've checked with our tax lawyers, and this prize is tax free. Of course, you'll have to fill out some tax forms at the end of the year, but we can help you with those."

"Ten million dollars a year!" The fact that I'd get this for not doing anything except letting the money sit in the bank made it feel like I had won not a hundred and eleven million dollars but a magic purse that always filled itself up again no matter how much you spent.

"Ok," I said, "I'll withdraw a hundred dollars."

Ms. Harrigan filled out a slip and stood up, indicating that our meeting was just about over.

"One more question, though," I said. "Mrs. Fordgythe, why did you deposit $110,999,997.46 instead of a hundred and eleven million?"

"Oh, my dear boy," she said, "Remember, you said that the ice cream float was on you."

Chapter 8

When I woke up the next day, I felt tired and restless, as if there were something I was supposed to be doing but I couldn't remember what. At first I thought it must have been a dream, but as I pulled on my clothing, it struck me: I had a hundred million dollars in the bank, and what I was supposed to do today was be rich.

The problem was that I had no idea how to be rich. I couldn't snap my fingers and have Jeeves the Butler enter. I couldn't go to the Rolls Royce store, pick out a model and say, "What the heck, give me two." I couldn't even buy a new basketball without making my parents suspicious.

I did figure out two things to do, although they'll probably seem awfully small to you – sort of pathetic, really. First, during lunch I bought an extra brownie. And then, after school, I went to the Small Lives pet store and got two fish I had been admiring for a long time but never even considered buying because they were way out of my price range. But my parents wouldn't know that. They had no idea how much fish cost, unless you're buying them by the pound.

My only fear was that they (my parents, not the fish) would ask me what I paid for them (the fish, not my parents). I promised myself that I would never lie about the money. I didn't want the money I'd won to turn me into a liar.

I emptied the baggie into the fish tank and watched my rare and exotic new fish examine their new home. They didn't seem to care at all. You've got to hand it to fish: It takes a lot to get them upset.

As I lay on my bed looking at the fish tank, I thought about how weird my day at school had been – my first day as a multi-millionaire. The day would go along normally and then I'd remember I was rich, and I'd get a little jolt. I'd drift off into a daydream for a bit, and then something would bring me back to school. I'd pay attention to school for a while, and then … another jolt.

I left my hundred dollars at home and went to school with three dollars in my backpack. They felt different now. Before, they were the three dollars that I had and everything I could buy was stacked up against them. Now, they were just a tiny part of an endless stream. It's like the difference between carrying a canteen and having running water. With a canteen you have to constantly worry about whether taking a drink now is going to mean you're going to go thirsty later. With running water, you just know it's always there. It's a good feeling.

But the most interesting thing that happened to me that day didn't seem that interesting at the time. It was Ari mooning about Amanda again. We were walking from English to Phys Ed (or "Fizz Ed" as I used to think it was called), the longest walk in the school. And since we were in the middle of a unit on aerobic exercises, neither of us was exactly racing to get there. I used to think running in place was the stupidest human activity, but then our class started doing "step aerobics" where you walk up and down a stairway that has a single step on it.

Ari was going on and on about how Amanda's hair smelled like roasted chestnuts and her smile was like square pearls with her braces being the necklace and her walk was like a gazelle except she only had two legs and didn't graze on wild clover or chew her cud.

This latest bout of Amanda fever was brought on by the fact that he had actually spoken with her. It took most of the walk to the gym to find out what had happened, but it seems that Ari had fallen off his skateboard just before entering the school building and, as luck would have it, was propelled straight into the school door precisely as Amanda was starting to enter. Ari rebounded off the door, and Amanda assumed that he was lunging to hold the door for her. She glanced at him and Ari, in his panic at being noticed, actually blurted out, "Terwilliger ..." It was the only word he could think of.

Amanda smiled the smile of a Greek goddess (remember, I heard this from Ari) and said, "Terwilliger? What about Terwilliger?"

"Spoon," Ari said.

"Yes it is. What do you know about it ... um ..." she said, pausing for him to tell her his name even though they had been in the same home room for four years and so she had heard his name called at roll approximately 720 times.

After a few moments in which Ari considered what it would take to get his name changed to "Rock" or "Lance," he said, "Ari."

"Well, Ari, how do you know about the Terwilliger Spoon?"

"I heard you lost it."

"From whom could you have heard such a thing?" she

asked, not so sweetly this time.

"From you. I was behind you when you were talking about it with Lydia."

"You were eavesdropping?"

"No. Well, yes, but not on purpose."

Amanda turned away and started walking down the hall. Desperate to extend the conversation, Ari blurted out, "I can help you find it."

"And how is that?"

"I think I know where it is."

"Where's that?"

"Um, the last place you saw it."

"At the Madagascar Café?"

"Yes, that's right, the Mada … Mada … Magadagga Daggadagga."

"Then why don't you get it for me?"

"Then you can go to the dance," Ari said hopefully.

But her eyes turned to weapons and she pierced him with her gaze. "I can go to any dance I want," she said icily.

"But I thought your father grounded you."

"That's what *he* thinks," she said. She lowered the flames in her eyes and said, suddenly sweetly, "But if you can get me the Terwilliger Spoon, I'd appreciate it." She smiled like a boa constrictor digesting a particularly juicy rabbit and walked slowly to her first class.

By the time I saw Ari during the walk to Fizz Ed, he was swinging back and forth between delight in thinking that Amanda had paid attention to him and fear that he had made a promise on which he could not come close to delivering.

"What am I going to do?" he said during one of the fearful moments. "I have no idea where the Terwilliger Spoon is."

"Well," I said, "she's given you a starting place. The Madagascar Café. Why don't we go over there this afternoon and see if they've found it?"

"Ok. But I wish she'd eaten somewhere easier to pronounce."

That afternoon, after I'd gone to the fish store and made my purchase – two Danio kyathi from Burma – Ari came over and we rode our bikes to the Madagascar. You could tell this was one of the fanciest restaurants in town because it only had a tiny sign. Also, there were real flowers in glass vases on top of white tablecloths on every table. This was definitely the type of place Amanda would hang out in. Of course, it didn't hurt that under the sign it said that it was "A Member of the Dunn Family of Companies" – yet another spot in town owned by Amanda's dad.

We stood outside, uncertain of how to approach the matter.

"We could just ask," I said.

"Ask if they found a fancy spoon? They'll know it's not ours."

"So? We'll tell them it's Amanda's and they'll call her

father."

"Then I won't get the credit. Besides, don't you think they would have noticed if they found a spoon? It must have gotten mixed up with their regular spoons which are probably pretty fancy themselves."

"We could ask to see their spoons," I said.

"Yeah, sure," Ari said sarcastically. "'We're teenage spoon inspectors. Show us your silverware or be prepared to suffer the consequences.'"

"Ok, ok," I said.

We stood silently, our bicycles leaning against us. "Got it!" I said. "You could get a job there washing dishes! Then you could inspect all the spoons."

Ari brightened. "Yeah!" he said enthusiastically. "Oh, no. Drat! How can I get a job there? My parents won't even let me join the computer club because I'm already doing too many things after school."

We pondered again. And thus it was that I ended up as the Madagascar's new dishwashing assistant.

This was not the way I had expected to spend my afternoons after I put $100,000,000 into my bank account.

It didn't take me long to be sure I had seen all of the restaurant's silverware. And all of it was the same. As far as I was concerned, there were only two types of silverware at Madagascar's: ones covered with goopy food, and ones clean but so hot that you could barely touch them.

I would have quit, but I would have felt like I had lied

to the manager of the Madagascar, a big man with a thin little mustache that fascinated me. Also, he turned out to be a pretty nice fellow. So I decided to stick it out there for a week.

When I was done, I reported to Ari that there was no Terwilliger Spoon there.

Ari wiped most of the milk off of his upper lip and said, "Well, that's that."

"Not necessarily," I said.

I had a plan. But I couldn't tell Ari because it would reveal to him that I was a rich kid. So, when he insisted on knowing, all I said was, "I can't tell you yet. But I'm going to need your help."

"Anything," he said, hope beginning to beat in his heart again.

"I need to find out exactly what the Terwilliger Spoon looked like."

"Why?"

"Just trust me."

"Well, ok," he said. "But how are we going to find out what it looked like?"

"Where else? The Internet."

Usually we're good at finding what we need – Ari especially has a knack for it – but we came up empty this time. So, that afternoon we went to the library, and we looked through just about every book and magazine in the place. We even engaged the help of Mr. Lipton the Librarian. He was a weight lifter and the rumor was that he had come in third in the Mr. Universe contest. When Mimi once asked him about it, he replied by giving her a Dewey Decimal number that turned out to lead to a shelf of books about rumors.

Mr. Lipton pointed Ari and me to reference works we had never even heard of. One weighed so much that it took two of us to open it, although Mr. Lipton carried it in one hand. All that we found was an entry in *The Century Book of Achievements* that was actually a guide to rich people. We discovered that Graham Terwilliger had made a fortune in India importing guns which he traded for Indian art masterpieces, and that he later settled in this country where he made a second fortune trading Indian masterpieces for logging rights in the Northwest. The only connection to a spoon was a reference to his elaborate parties. Perhaps he used the spoon to serve caviar ... which he probably served in crumpled up Indian art masterpieces.

We left the library no wiser – at least, not any wiser about the Terwilliger Spoon.

Ari, predictably, was glum. I said, "Let's go to the Soda Squirt."

"I'm out of money," said Ari. "I spent everything on a new pair of shoes for the dance."

"That's ok, I think I have some," I said. "You know, from washing dishes at The Madagascar." I'd earned $54 from my work. When I'd gone to deposit it, Ms. Minden took me aside, punched some numbers into a calculator, and told me that in the nine hours I'd worked at The Madagascar, I'd earned $4,109.59 in interest, just by doing nothing. That's $684.93

every hour of nothingness.

While we were slurping the last of the chocolate glop at the bottom of our Atomic Sundaes, I had an idea.

"What is it?" Ari asked.

"I'll tell you. And the best part is, you get to speak to Amanda again."

So, the next day, Ari showed up at school forty-five minutes before it started so that he could casually run into Amanda by coincidental unplanned accident. I sat with him behind a large tree at the end of the schoolyard where we had a strategic view of everyone who entered. I had a nasty cramp by the time Amanda strolled up the stairs, and wasn't really paying attention. And Ari was busy trying to carve his and Amanda's initials into the bark of the tree with a number 2 pencil. When I spotted her, it was almost too late. Ari shot up like a rabbit who's just seen a fox, and practically knocked Amanda down. Again.

Because we had gone over what he was going to say so many times, I could tell what he was saying even though I could only barely hear him: "Hey, Amanda, I had an idea. If your father has a picture of the Terwilliger Spoon, I'd be happy to make some inquiries." This would have come off as more casual if he hadn't had to look twice at a scrap of paper he was carrying to remind himself of what he was supposed to say.

There followed an exchange I couldn't make out, but apparently it went well enough because Ari came back and reported that she was going to think about it.

The next day, Ari found an envelope in his locker with a

picture of the Terwilliger Spoon inside it.

And at last I had found a reason to be rich.

• • •

I rode to the edge of town where there was a shop I had often passed and wondered about: Smithy's Silver Smith. The store's neighbors were a bingo parlor and an abandoned tire store with a pile of old tires in the parking lot. There, between them, was Smithy's, with a carefully cleaned blue and silver sign picturing a gleaming crown. In the window were shiny rings, broaches and necklaces, carefully arranged on black velvet. It seemed an odd place to have a silver shop,

"Hello?" the owner asked, not looking up from the stool on which he sat. He was hunched over a work table that had strands of wire, pliers, a lit flame, small hammers, and polishing cloths.

"Hello," I said.

"Ah, a child," he said, still not looking up.

"Yeah, I guess."

"He guesses!" he said, snorting a laugh. He looked up. "Ah, an in-betweener," he said, not unkindly. He was holding a battered piece of silver with a dark pair of pliers in one hand, and a sharp-pointed hammer in the other. He put them both down, dropped off the stool – his feet didn't reach the ground while sitting – brushed some silvery slivers from his thick brown apron, and looked me straight in the eye.

"How can I help you, my young man," he asked.

"Do you make silver things?"

He gestured to his work bench. "That is precisely what I do. Guillermo Smith, silversmith," he said, shaking my hand. He looked me in the eye again, as if trying to see something buried way back in my brain, as I waited for sensation to return to my crumpled right hand. His own eyes were dark and capped by bushy eyebrows that needed a good mowing. The rest of his head was hairless.

After staring into my face, he seemed to make up his mind about me. "How can I help?"

"Can you make a spoon for me?"

"A spoon?" he asked thoughtfully. "Yes, well, of course."

"Except it's got to look just like this," I said, pulling out the picture of the Mr. Dunn's spoon.

"The Terwilliger," he said.

"You know it?"

"Yes, I know it. My father made it."

"Really?"

"Really. He was commissioned to make twenty of them. I watched him make them as a boy."

"That's amazing," I said. "But I thought it was commissioned by a guy who lived in the 19th Century."

He laughed. "That was the story the man who created them wanted people to believe. He was really just a local businessman with an eye for a sharp deal. He thought it would make the spoons more valuable if they had a glamorous history. It worked, too. He made a fortune selling them to collectors."

"But they're not really worth that much?"

"Oh, don't get me wrong. My father did a magnificent job on them. They just have nothing to do with Indians and elephants. But the Terwilligers are special to me. They're what got me interested in silver smithing. I watched my father craft each one to perfection. I loved everything about them – the brightness of the silver, the tapping and tinking of the hammer, the shine that came out of hiding if you rubbed it enough. My father was a far better silversmith than I."

"Do you think you could make another?"

"Perhaps. I don't know. I'd like to try. But why would you want a Terwilliger Spoon?"

I remembered my vow not to let my fortune turn me into a liar. "I can't really tell you," I said. He nodded, turned his back to me, and bent over his workbench. "But I promise you, it's not for anything wrong."

"Can you tell me what you would do with it?"

"I'm going to replace one that a friend lost."

"Hmm. I'm not sure."

"It's not like I'm going to sell it to make money. I just want to help out a friend."

"Do you have any idea how much it would cost to make a spoon like the Terwilliger?" I shook my head. "It's a big spoon. Lots of silver. Highest quality. That itself will run hundreds of dollars. And then you'll only have a shapeless lump of metal." He looked to see if I was shocked. "Then, I'll have to spend many, many hours working the metal. Look at the detail in this photograph. All told, I'd say it's going to cost around $2,000. So, much as I'd like to help you ..."

I took out an envelope from my backpack and started counting out hundred dollar bills; I had stopped at the bank on my way over. When I got to 20, I stopped counting. "That's two thousand," I said.

I must say I enjoyed Mr. Smith's look of astonishment.

"Where on earth did you ..."

Now it was my turn to look Mr. Smith in the eye. I made a decision. "I can trust you can't I?"

"Yes," he said. I liked that he didn't say anything more.

"I won a lot of money in the state lottery. But no one knows because I can't tell my parents about it."

"You won enough to afford spending $3,000 on an ugly ceremonial spoon?"

"I thought you said it was $2,000."

"That was before I knew you could afford it."

Mr. Smith looked lovingly at the photograph. "A Terwilliger. It's something I've always wanted to try. Come back in a week."

Chapter 9

Ari, Mimi and I went to the movies the next night. The line was long and when we finally got to the ticket booth, Ari started fishing through his pockets, trying to find enough coins to pay. He pulled out old LifeSavers, a bubble gum wrapper, a rusty AA battery, a button declaring him a Special Saver at the local drug store, and more shredded tissues than anyone should have to look at. I was tempted to whip open my wallet, slap a fifty dollar bill down, and pay for all three of us.

But I couldn't. I had to pretend to be a kid with only a kid's amount of money.

Then we went to the snack counter. Mimi ordered a large popcorn and a small soda. It was $6.50. She only had $6, so she had to have the guy take back the popcorn and get a medium. Meanwhile, I'm standing there with enough money in my pocket to buy snacks for the entire line. I wanted to be able to say to her, "Get whatever you want. It's on me." But I couldn't. She turned down my offer of fifty cents but if she knew I had $100,000,000 I think she would have been OK with it.

The next day the three of us were in a bookstore because Mimi had to buy a copy of *David Copperfield*, part of the Read Books You Don't Like program in school. We were browsing, and she was thumbing through a book about the history of comics and their relationship to the historical events of the time. It looked great but it cost $35 so Mimi wasn't even thinking about buying it. But could I say, "Let's get it and then look around for more books that seem interesting"? Nope. I couldn't even buy her the hardcover version of *David Copperfield* even though Mimi always says how much she prefers hard covers to paperbacks.

I had been able to buy myself two tropical fish. That's what my $100,000,000 had been good for so far.

It was driving me nuts.

• • •

At our next band rehearsal, we were still totally terrible. But occasionally we would accidentally hit the right note at the same time and it would sound good. There is something special about playing music together that I don't think you can understand until you've done it. A sound comes out that needed three people to be heard, if only for one second.

That happened maybe twice. The rest of the time we played our instruments, made jokes, tried out different ways of arranging the songs, drank soda, and were silly.

And then while Ari was coming out of a big drum solo that sounded like someone had rolled a drum set down a stairway, Mimi started playing her bass guitar. After four measures, I was supposed to come in with my guitar. But just as Mimi was hitting the lowest note her guitar makes, the sound from her lousy amplifier went from really bad to not even being music. You know those noisemakers you blow through and they make a razzing noise? That's what Mimi's amplifier now sounded like. She tried playing high notes and the razzing sounded more duck-like. Since we knew of no bands that have been successful by playing the electric duck, we stopped and considered the possibilities.

"It doesn't sound good," I noted cleverly.

"It sounds way broken," Ari said.

"Maybe it's just a loose wire or something," Mimi said hopefully, unplugging it from the wall. "Do you have a screw driver?"

"Give it a minute," I said. "Sometimes electrical stuff stores electricity."

"I'm just going to take off the front," she said. Ari handed her a screwdriver. The front cover came off easily. "Well, that's not good," Mimi said, pointing to a large rip in the paper speaker.

"We could tape it," Ari said.

"I don't think so," I said. But we tried anyway. Now the amplifier sounded like a duck with a cork in its bill.

"What are we going to do?" Mimi asked? "That was my brother's amp."

"Is he going to be angry?"

"No, he hasn't played in years. He pretty much gave it to me. But I can't afford to replace it."

The magic words: "Can't afford." They were magic because they stopped people from doing things. But I had bigger magic. Much bigger.

"I may have money saved up..." I began.

Mimi looked at me sharply. "I thought you said you had about $50 a couple of weeks ago. Besides, I wouldn't let you buy me a new amp. They cost hundreds of dollars."

"Well," said Ari, "I guess that's the end of The Scutters." He put his drumsticks down. "Too bad. We were getting really good."

No, we weren't, but why argue?

"Well, I was going to have to return my drum set soon anyway," Ari said. His parents had rented it for him to try out.

"So," said Mimi, "Let's see. We have one drummer playing the air drums, one bass player playing the ripped-speaker amp, and one lead guitarist with a toy amplifier." I was using an amp designed for little kids who wanted to pretend that they're on the radio. "Quite the Top 40 group." She packed her bass into its cardboard carrying case.

"Are you quitting?"

"I'm not quitting, but I can't play if my amplifier sounds like the back end of a cow with indigestion."

"Ewwww," said Ari. "Once I was visiting a farm with my parents and…"

"Ok, Ari, we don't have to hear about that," said Mimi, who really had no one to blame but herself for bringing it up in the first place.

Mimi headed toward the door. "I guess I'll go home and get ahead on my homework or something."

"Can you wait a minute?" I asked.

"Sure. You want to ride with me?"

"No. I mean, I'm not sure. Can you just give me a minute

to think?"

"Well, goll-lee!" Mimi said, surprised at the sharpness in my tone. Usually when people say, "Can you give me a minute to think?" what they actually mean is, "Back off! You're rushing me." But I actually wanted a minute to think.

It's hard to think when your friends are watching you. How do you sit in a thinkful position? How do you stroke your beard if you don't have one? I felt them looking at me, wondering what I was thinking about. Of course, mainly I was thinking about how hard it is to think when people are watching you try to think.

So I gave up thinking and instead decided.

"I'll get you a new amplifier," I said.

"With what? Fifty dollars? That's very nice of you, Jake, but …"

"No, I'll get you whatever amplifier you want."

"Ok, I'd like a Fender 810 Pro cabinet with, oh, let's see, a Fender Bassman 300 All Tube head."

"Ok."

"That'll run you, let's see, that's $1,000 and $1,100, a total of about $2,100."

"Ok."

"Ok?"

"Well, not entirely ok."

"Aha," Mimi said. "I didn't think so!"

"But the money is ok."

"The money is ok?"

"The money is ok."

"So, what isn't ok?" she asked.

"You can't get anything too obvious."

"A Fender 810 Pro with a Bassman 300 All Tube head is pretty obvious."

"That's the problem," I said.

Ari interrupted. "Could you two please talk in longer sentences?"

"Yeah," said Mimi, "and maybe you could explain what the heck you're talking about."

"Sit down, Mimi," I said, patting the couch next to me. "Really, you want to be sitting for this."

She didn't look happy about being told what to do. But she sat down anyway. "I'm sitting. Go ahead."

"I won the lottery."

"Hey, that's great!" said Ari.

"Congratulations," Mimi said. "Do your parents know?"

"Nope. I haven't told them."

"You're lying to them?"

"No, I just haven't told them."

"Interesting. So, how much did you win?" Mimi asked.

"A lot."

"A lot a lot?" asked Ari.

"More than a lot a lot."

"How much more?" Mimi asked.

"$100,000,000."

Mimi laughed once. Ari seemed to lose interest. He was assuming that I was teasing. "No, really," she said.

"$100,000,000."

"Uh huh. How much, Jake?"

"You're right. It wasn't $100,000,000. It was $111,000,000, but I gave $11,000,000 to Maddie because I promised her 10% if she'd keep it quiet."

Mimi laughed harder. Ari looked angry. "Why don't you just tell us?" he demanded.

"It's true. I was the big winner."

"You bought a ticket even though your father is the biggest anti-lottery guy in the state?" Mimi asked.

"You never buy tickets," Ari pointed out.

"Not exactly." And then I told them how by being a nice boy I'd been given a ticket by a lady who looked like a spaceship and how I was hiding it from my parents and how I'd bought two tropical fish.

"That's great," Mimi said, "but I don't actually believe you."

"Me neither."

"Me neither," I said. "I wake up every day and I check to

see whether it's still true. And it is."

"Prove it," Ari said. He didn't like being teased.

"How?"

"Buy something. Something big and expensive."

"I can't. I have to pay in cash because I don't have a credit card. And I can't buy anything that my parents can find out about because then they'll know. And you guys can't tell anyone!"

"Don't worry," said Mimi. "We don't believe you enough to tell anyone."

"But when you do believe me..."

"Then we both promise never to say a word. Don't we, Ari?"

"Yeah, sure, I guess."

"You can't guess. You have to promise," I said.

"All right. I promise not to tell anyone your fake secret. It's not very nice, you know, Jake."

"Sorry but it's true. Tomorrow let's go shopping for bass amps. And I'll get me a new guitar."

Ari looked hurt. "How about something for me?"

"That's going to be tough. I can buy an amp for Mimi and a guitar for me because we'll keep them here in your basement and your parents won't notice or think anything of it. But if you were to come home with a brand new, fancy drum set, how would you explain it to your parents?"

"I found it?"

"We'll have to try to think of something to buy you that your parents won't notice."

"Oh. Good! ... Not that I believe you," Ari said.

"No, of course not."

The next day after school, the three of us went to the outskirts of town where there was a store that sold musical instruments. It was one of those stores that looked like it was owned by someone who really loved what they sold. New and used instruments were stacked everywhere: brass over here, woodwinds over there, keyboards in the back. A guy was playing some pretty great guitar in the big area lined with guitars of all sorts. He finished the line of music he was playing, put the guitar down, and said "Just looking or can I help you?"

This was the moment. Mimi and Ari had come along with me, playing it safe by pretending I was fooling them. But they also knew me well enough to know that I wouldn't lead a salesperson along only to reveal at the end that we were really just wasting his time.

It should have been easy. After all, we *were* there to buy. I'd taken $5,000 out of the bank account. Fifty hundred dollar bills were in an envelope in my backpack. So, all I had to say was, "We'd like to buy an amp and a guitar."

But I hesitated. I looked around. I cleared my throat. I said "um" a couple of times just to make it clear that I was still paying attention. I checked to see if my shoes needed tying.

"Make yourself at home," the man said. "Try out anything you want."

So we did. I took down an expensive electric guitar. "Let me plug that in for you," the man said. "I know some stores tell kids not to touch. But it's my store and playing music means touching an instrument just right. That's what I always say. Here you go." Not only did he plug the guitar into an amplifier, he turned it up loud. Very loud. So loud that even my lousy playing sounded good. Every note I played caused every other instrument in the place to vibrate at the same frequency. From alto saxes and bass drums to xylophones and zithers, they all were playing along with me. I wasn't playing the guitar. I was playing a music store.

It was the best I'd ever played.

After the vibrating and echoing had ended, the store owner said, "Cool, isn't it?" and I could only nod in reply.

"How about a bass amplifier," Mimi prodded me.

"Ok," I said. "Excuse me, but do you have any bass amplifiers?"

"Sure we do. New and used. Come over here. And take down one of those bass guitars so you can try them out."

Mimi selected a cheap one. "I don't want to scratch it and have to buy it," she explained to me.

The man picked out a big old bass amp and plugged Mimi in. And he turned it up loud. Everything shook. If Mimi had found the right notes, she probably could have hopped the entire store over a couple of feet.

"That's an old one," the man said, "but I like it better than most of the new ones. Very rich, bass-y bass."

Mimi nodded, overwhelmed. "It's bass-y all right."

"Try out some of the others if you want," the man said.

"I love this one. It's old and it's beat up, but the sound is amazing."

"Good," I said. "Ari's parents are less likely to notice a used one than if we came in with a new one. So, should we get it?"

"Yeah, sure," Mimi said, not sure if she was serious or just playing along with a joke.

"Ok. And I'd like to get myself a guitar."

"Sure," Mimi said. "How about this one? It's only ..." she looked at the price tag, "$1,500."

"Yeah, I like that one. But this one feels better," I said, handing her a beautiful new guitar with a bright orange sunburst finish.

"And it's only $1,250. What a bargain."

"I think so, too. I'm going to get it."

"Great. And I'll buy you a flat pick for it. Just to keep up my end. What do they cost these days? Twenty-five cents? Heck, I'll get you two."

"Can I get these drumsticks?" Ari asked.

"Get a dozen of 'em," I said.

"Ok, big shot," said Mimi. "Go up to the nice man and buy the guitar, the bass amp, and the half dozen drumsticks."

"And the flat pick," Ari said.

So I gathered my courage and went up to the man. "Excuse me, but we'd like to buy some stuff."

"Sure," he said. "What'll it be?"

"Well, this is going to seem strange, but I was given a lot of money for a big event..."

"Like a birthday?" he suggested.

"Sort of. So, I have a whole bunch of cash, and I'd like to buy..." and then I just blurted it out: "This bass amp, this guitar and a dozen drumsticks."

"And a flat pick," said Ari.

"Have you seen the price tags?" the man asked.

"Yes. The guitar is $1,250 and the bass amp is $650. And the drumsticks are $5 each." I reached into my backpack and took out twenty bills. "And this is our money."

"Whoa!" the man said, surprised I actually had the cash.

"Oh my gosh!" Mimi said.

The man drummed his fingers on the counter. "Usually when a kid is given a bunch of money for his birthday or his bar mitzvah or whatever it was, and he wants to spend it on instruments, his parents come in with him," he said.

"I'm sure," I said. "But this is different. My parents would be fine with it."

"I believe you, but I have to check with them."

"Why?"

"Look at it from my point of view. I trust you. I like you. I watched how you treated each other. You're good friends and that means you're good kids."

"Thank you."

"But, I can't take $2,000 from a kid who's, what, 13 or 14 years old. Suppose it's money his parents gave him for college. He brings his equipment home and I get an angry call from his parents. How dare I take that money from a kid? Didn't I know better? I've got to give the money back, and I'm lucky if the parents don't call the police on me. You understand?"

"I guess."

"Look, I feel terrible. I'd love for you to have the instruments. I'd love to make the money selling them to you. But I can't. Not like this. Bring your parents in and we'll do it."

"Are you sure?"

"I'm sure. I'm sorry but I'm sure."

I must have looked as sad as I felt. I liked that guitar a lot, and I wanted Mimi to have her bass amp. The man saw how I was feeling and said, "I won't sell the amp or the guitar to anyone until you come back. Any time in the next week. Ok? Then you can bring your mom or dad in..."

I wasn't going to be bringing my parents in. "Thanks, but don't bother."

"Ok. Whatever you say. Sorry, kids."

"Us, too. But thanks for letting us play. You have a very cool store."

"Thanks. Come back again."

As we were getting on our bikes, Mimi said to me, "That was hard. We believe you."

"Yeah," said Ari. "You won the lottery."

"I only wish we could celebrate," I said. And then we rode home to Ari's garage, my cheap guitar, and Mimi's broken amp.

Chapter 10

"Keep it down," my father yelled at me from another room.

I was shocked.

My father was being really, really crabby. Normally, my father is, if anything, a goofball, the type of dad who balances a round cushion on his head while dancing around the room singing "It's Only a Paper Moon," for no reason at all. When he gets angry, it's usually because of something particular. Then he confronts you with it in person, you get punished if that's required, and it's over and he's back to being his normal goofball self. Oh, sometimes he gets a little overly-serious about some issue, but that's Dad being a newspaper editor.

So I was surprised when he yelled at me for singing along to an MP3 in my room. Sure, I may have hit some remarkable high notes that went through our house's walls like a hot skewer going through a marshmallow. But normally my father would have joined in instead of yelling at me. Worse, he was staying mad. When I went into the study where he was working on something on his computer, he didn't look up and didn't say hello. He was being crabby.

The next morning at breakfast, he was a big bowl full of crabs again. He stood by the counter reading the paper – not *The Gaz*, but the big city paper we had delivered – and only talked to us to get us to eat more neatly, which is usually my mother's job. It was as if he were looking for ways to crab us out.

That afternoon, he drove me to the dentist. In silence. As we pulled into the parking lot, I asked him "What's wrong?"

He still didn't look at me. "Nothing's wrong," he said, but he must have sounded unconvincing even to himself. "I'm having a little trouble with the paper."

"What kind of trouble? Can I help?"

"No," he answered, almost smiling. "It's nothing to worry about. It's just that advertising is down."

"Why?"

"Competition. *The Boynton County Register* is eating into *The Gaz* a little bit. It's just part of business."

"*The Register?* Why would anyone advertise there?"

"They cover a lot more territory. Of course, they don't cover it as well, but advertisers like having their message delivered all over the tri-county area."

"What are you going to do?"

"There's not much to do. We'll do fine," he said, trying to look unconcerned. But I had a full day of his crabbiness behind me to tell me that he was worried.

After the dentist, I met up with Ari. He was putting decals on his skateboard. "Aren't they cool?" he asked. I agreed, although I thought what would really make him look cool on a skateboard was not falling off of it every time he got on it.

"So, were you kidding about the lottery?"

"No."

"That is so cool."

"Yeah, I guess."

"Can we, like, go buy something?"

"No, Ari," I said, getting a little crabby myself. "I told you, no one can know about this." A sudden suspicion came over me. "Did you tell anyone?"

"No!" he insisted convincingly. "Hey, Mimi," he said, waving to her as she zoomed up on her bike.

"Hey, rich boy," she said.

"Mimi! Don't tease me. That has to stay really secret."

"Ok," she said. "I won't ever call you that again." And she didn't.

"Hey," I said, "I have to show you something." I took the new Terwilliger Spoon out of its velvet sack.

"Wow," Ari and Mimi said together.

Ari broke the silence. "How much...?" he asked.

"You're looking at three thousand dollars worth of spoon."

"That's a lot of spoon," Mimi said. She cocked her head to the side to get a new look at it. "It's kind of ugly."

She was right. Too many curlicues for my taste.

"So, how are we going to give it to Amanda?" Ari asked.

"I'm not sure," I said. "Maybe after school you could go up to her..."

"Go up to her?" he said with fear written across his face in big red letters.

"No," said Mimi with certainty, "I think we ought to go for drama here." Ari put down the rag he was using to wipe the dirt off his skateboard. "She'll like that better. Don't just *give* it to her. Make it reappear mysteriously, and let her know that you're the one that made it happen."

"Interesting," I said. "What's your plan?"

• • •

"So," said Ari to Amanda, one foot nervously rolling his skateboard backwards and forwards. In my head I was yelling, "Get your foot off the skateboard!" I knew what would happen.

"So what?" replied Amanda, not particularly warmly.

"So, I was just wondering if your father has a special place for the Terwilliger Spoon."

Amanda looked at him as if he were from another planet. I couldn't blame her. Although Ari was following our script, he was so awkward and phony about it that he did seem a bit like an alien trying to pass for human. "Why do you care?" she asked in return.

"Just idly wondering. No real reason. Just wondering. Wondering, wondering …"

Lydia, standing next to Amanda, said to her, "Come on, let's go."

"He keeps it on the mantel in the drawing room, if you really want to know" Amanda said.

"Mantel, mantel. Very mantle. Yes, drawing roomly mantel. Very mantel-y." Ari's circuits obviously were melting down.

Fortunately, Lydia stepped in and pulled Amanda away as she stared at my gibbering friend.

As was inevitable, the skateboard slipped from under Ari's foot, bounced off the wall, and skittered to a stop at the bottom of the hill. Fortunately, it hadn't actually run anyone over. This time.

"Good job," I said to Ari after the two girls had left.

"Mantle-y," he replied.

Thus concluded Phase One of Mimi's plan, also known as The Easy Phase.

• • •

Phase Two promised to bring much more adventure. Somehow, we had to sneak the spoon back into the Dunn Mansion.

Mimi had worked out the details. That's why I was now drinking more water than I could possible hold, waiting for Amanda to enter the cafeteria. At last, water burbling out of my mouth back into the water bubbler as quickly as it was burbling in, Amanda and Lydia approached. I casually followed them into the cafeteria and sat down next to them.

"Mind if I sit here," I said, already sitting.

"Well..." began Lydia.

"It's a free country," finished Amanda. Charming girls.

I put my book bag next to Amanda's. And waited.

We were half way through the green Jell-O with mystery fruit before Mimi sauntered up. Lydia had left for her next class.

"Amanda, can I talk with you for a minute?" Mimi asked.

Amanda looked surprised. Then annoyed. "I'm eating," she replied, gently nibbling around the Jell-O edges of what once might have been a grape.

"It's important. It'd be a personal favor."

You could almost hear Amanda's inner voice thinking, "Aha! She'll owe me a favor in return … something I can use against her whenever I want!" "Well, ok," she said out loud. "Go ahead."

"Not here. It's personal. Could you just step over to this empty table?"

While they were chatting, I managed to "accidentally" knock both my bag and Amanda's onto the floor. While scrabbling under the table to retrieve both bags, I replaced Amanda's social studies book with my own. We were done with social studies for the day and I hoped she wouldn't notice the switch before she got home.

I was just bringing the bags back up to the table when Amanda came back.

"What are you doing?" she demanded.

"Our bags fell off. Just picking them up. Sorry."

Amanda looked darts at me, took one more spoon of green Jell-O, and left for English class.

When she was safely gone, Mimi came over. "You do it?" she asked.

"Yup. What did you two gals talk about?"

"Oh, nothing."

"It had to be something."

"Just girl talk."

"Girl talk? I didn't know there still was something called girl talk."

"If you must know, I asked her advice. I figured it would appeal to her vanity."

"Advice on what."

"Nothing."

"Something. What was it?

"Well," Mimi said, flushing, "If you really have to know, I asked her if she was interested in you. You know, if that's why she was sitting next to you. I acted jealous."

"No!"

"Absolutely. And she fell for it."

"Really?"

"She didn't suspect a thing."

I picked up my book bag – the one with Amanda's book in it – and started to go to my next class. But I turned and asked Mimi one more question: "What did she say about being interested in me?"

The answer apparently involved Mimi dumping the last of the green Jell-o into my hair.

• • •

On a normal Saturday, I'd be in my worst jeans, which are,

of course, the ones I like best – ripped knees, a patch where the back pocket used to be, cuffs torn up and greasy from getting caught in my bike chain. Not this Saturday, though. No, I was dressed better than I dress for school. I even combed my hair with water so that it would stay in place for more than 12 minutes. Today was special. Today, I was going to the Palace of the Dunns.

At 12:30, Ari pulled up to our house. He was not only dressed neatly, he actually had buttoned his top button, making him look like he had escaped from a 1950s sitcom. He was fidgeting, scratching at his arms then his ribs, then his arms again. Meanwhile, he had a dumb grin stuck on his face.

"Let's go," I said, and we rode off to the Dunns' house.

You could see the house towering over Chestnut Hill as you rode up. First you saw the twin towers, covered with ivy. Then you saw the main part of the house, three stories, old brick, stained glass windows. Then at last you saw the tall iron gate with the steel muskrats atop every post. We announced ourselves at the gate to a man twice my father's age and with twice my father's hair. "You are expected," he said after looking at a list on a clipboard. The gate swung open and we bicycled in.

As we walked up the steps, the door opened as if by magic. The front hall was the size of a small circus tent, with wood and stained glass everywhere. A stairway wide enough for three horses swept through the center. The hall was colder than outside and smelled like my grandmother's linen closet. Behind the door was a tall man who introduced himself as Mr. Paul and offered us lemonade. I said yes at the same time as

Ari said no. Ari switched to yes.

As Mr. Paul's footsteps echoed behind him, we heard the soft shuffle of slippers. Who was approaching but Mr. Dunn himself, dressed in a dark blue business suit, white shirt, yellow tie with blue stripes, and worn-out leather slippers. He had a copy of *The Register* folded under one arm with a copy of *The Gaz* sticking out from inside of it. "Who have we here?" he asked in a courteous voice. "Friends of Amanda's?"

"Yes, sir," I said. I don't usually call people "sir," but I had a sense that Mr. Dunn would like it. "I'm Jake and this is Ari."

Mr. Dunn shook our hands. "Mr. Paul has let you in and is fetching Amanda?"

"Lemonade," Ari said.

"Ah, yes, lemonade. And Amanda. And do you have last names?"

"Richter," I said. If I'd made up a name to protect my identity, I was sure that Ari would have corrected me.

"Jake Richter," Mr. Dunn said thoughtfully. He straightened the papers under his arm so that *The Gaz* no longer stuck out. I couldn't tell whether that was because he recognized me as the son of the editor of his competitor or because he saw me staring at the papers. "And you, my boy?" he asked Ari.

"Ari," he said again.

"And your last name?"

Ari said nothing for a suspiciously long time. "Marshall," I said.

"Mr. Marshall, you might want to study a bit harder," Mr. Dunn said in what was apparently supposed to be a joke. "Next time, we'll have a pop quiz."

"Pop," Ari said.

Then it became clear why Ari had been left speechless: Amanda had entered from the library, a blaze of red and orange in a house of brown and black. "Ah, there she is. Enjoy this glorious afternoon," Mr. Dunn said.

Amanda was carrying my social studies book, the one I'd switched with hers in the cafeteria on Friday. Ari looked at her like a bird that's just been shot out of a tree. But before he hit ground he saw another person enter from the library: Roger. The football player. Roger. The boyfriend. You could practically see Ari shrink inside his clothes.

As Roger was looking us up and down, no doubt figuring how many yards he could throw us, Mr. Paul came back with four glasses and a pitcher on a silver tray. "Shall I serve the lemonade on the veranda, Amanda?" Although I was tempted to reply, "How about in the hall, Mr. Paul?" I was a good boy and held myself back. Amanda was surprised that we were staying longer than it took just to drop off the book, but she had been brought up to be polite enough not to object as we walked to a porch full of tropical flowers and the tinkle of falling water. Not exactly my taste, but not half bad.

"This is an amazing house," I said.

"It's a total pain to live in," said Amanda. "You can't leave your stuff around, and if you should happen to get lipstick on the crystal mirrors in the ballroom, well, you have to spend all

afternoon cleaning it off. And the heater in the pool breaks."
Poor, poor Amanda.

If I could spend my money openly and decided to build a house, I would use Amanda's mansion as a guide to my architect. I'd take him on a tour and point out the various features: "Not like this. And not like this. And definitely not like this."

Ari was gulping his lemonade down, as if being in the presence of Amanda was like getting too close to the sun and had dried out his body. I motioned to him to slow down. Our plan required us to spend a few minutes in the house. "Would you mind if I used your bathroom?" I asked. Amanda rolled her eyes. "It's that way," she said, pointing in the direction away from the library with its mantel-y mantel.

I left Ari sitting at the table as Roger smirked and Amanda put her tanned legs up on the chair opposite her. I was worried that this might be too much for my friend, but I had no choice. The Plan required it.

The bathroom was about the size of my bedroom. After standing there for a moment, inspecting the lion-headed faucet and the framed photograph of Mr. Dunn shaking hands with the president of either some large corporation or some small country, I left the bathroom and purposefully went wrong. After a few minutes of wandering, I made my way into the library and, slipping my Terwilliger Spoon out of its velvet sack, placed it onto the mantel of the library in the stand that had been created especially for it. It looked perfect, the silver shining like a spark of fire in its mahogany frame. Mission accomplished.

"May I help you?" came the voice behind me. I whirled around. Mr. Paul had just entered.

"No, I'm just trying to find my way back to the veranda. And Amanda," I said. "Which way is the hall, Mr. Paul?" I'd resisted the first time, but couldn't help myself the second.

"To your left, go straight, turn right at the potting room, and the veranda is right there." After I thanked him, he said, "Don't break the rake, Jake."

Maybe he was ok.

When I rejoined the awkward little party, Amanda was putting some type of oil on her legs. Roger was spitting ice cubes at a garden gnome. Ari was breathing heavily, as if trying to inhale Amanda through his nose. I nodded at Ari, our signal that all had gone well and said, "Well, we should be going. Let's exchange books and we'll be on our way." Amanda slid my book over to me and I gave her hers. This was Ari's cue.

He, of course, didn't take it. He sat there like a dog with its head out the window of a car, his tongue flapping in the breeze. "We'll be on our way," I said again, pointedly. More silence. "There's just one more thing," I said, stealing Ari's line, hoping to jump start him. "Isn't there just one more thing, Ari?" Ari was supposed to say, "If you check your library, you'll find the Terwilliger Spoon." Instead Ari said, "One more thing? What?"

Amanda interrupted our stumbling little script. "Oh," she said, "by the way, we found that stupid Terwilliger Spoon thing."

Of course it was that moment that Ari chose to speak his

lines: "If you check your library, you'll find the Terwilliger Spoon."

"Yes, I know," Amanda said, looking at him as if he were an idiot, which, technically speaking, he was being. "We found it last week behind a couch in the home theatre. It was just a little scratched and dusty, but Mr. Paul's been fixing it up."

And what exactly would Mr. Paul – and Amanda – and Amanda's father! – say when they found a second Terwilliger Spoon proudly displayed in their library? We had to grab the spoon before anyone noticed.

Ari, having gotten started on his scripted speech, was continuing to give it. "You see," he said, "We recovered your spoon …"

"Ari," I said sharply, "I know you're excited that Amanda's family found the spoon. Very excited. But there's no need to go on about it."

"But…" said Ari.

"No buts. We really should be going. Must be going. Must must." Then I had an idea. "Say, when do you think Mr. Paul will be finished fixing up that old spoon. We'd love to see it. Heard so much about it and all."

"Oh, I don't know," said Amanda, without really thinking. "I think he was working on it this morning."

"Ooh," I said, clutching my stomach. "Stomach ache! Can I borrow your bathroom again."

Amanda rolled her eyes. "Whatever."

I headed down the hall to the library but made a sharp left

when I saw Mr. Paul approaching from the opposite direction. I was now in unexplored territory. At the end of the long corridor was some type of big room with ceilings high enough to let you raise a family of falcons. My chances of being discovered were much greater in a room that large and open, so I ducked up a small stairway to my left. Although it wasn't disguised or camouflaged, the stairs were so dark that they might as well have been hidden. I walked up carefully, trying to keep my feet on the edge of each step because I read in a spy book that that's how you keep stairs from creaking. The spy book was wrong. But I made it to the top undiscovered.

And there was Mr. Dunn's private study. I knew it was Mr. Dunn's because there were pictures of him on every wall: photos with the mayor, our senator, and with three former presidents, an oil painting of him standing like a king with one hand on a globe, and photos from newspaper stories about his successes. I knew it was private because there was only one chair in it, a green leather one the size of a throne behind the desk. What surprised me was that, based on the Web page open on his computer screen, Mr. Dunn was looking into buying a dune buggy. This was a house of surprises.

I crept out of the room as quietly as I could and came back down the dark stairway. By my reckoning, if I took a series of right turns, I should have ended up back in the library. But my reckoning isn't very good when it comes to directions. In fact, I once got lost in my own house, although my parents had switched some pictures around so maybe it's not as bad as it sounds. No, it is as bad as it sounds.

After a series of right turns down big corridors, I found

myself not in the library but at a door to the greenhouse…a large, glass-lined dead end. I turned around and saw what could only be Mr. Paul's workroom. The door was open and the light was off. It was a small room, but bigger than Mr. Dunn's private office. Mr. Paul apparently was quite the handyman, for the walls were lined with tools for working with wood, for fixing electronics, for shaping metal and for fiddling with small mechanisms like watches. And there, in the middle of the worktable at the center of the room was the Terwilliger Spoon, as shiny and Terwilliger-y as ever.

I heard footsteps.

I moved in one step and pretended to be looking around for the exit even though it was right behind me.

The footsteps turned a corner and got softer and softer.

Afraid that I might be found at any moment, without thinking I swiped the Spoon and left.

With it safe in my pocket, I made my way back to the veranda where Ari was rocking back and forth on his feet, like a tuning fork. He was apparently trying to have a relaxed conversation with Amanda. "Hey," I said, "We'd better be going."

"Going. Got to going. Going," said Ari.

Amanda barely looked up as she said, "Really? So soon? Well, bye bye. Mr. Paul will see you out."

And so we left that house of many corridors and too many spoons. When we were back on the street, at the end of the long path from their house and safely out of view, I reached into my pocket and pulled out the Terwilliger Spoon triumphantly. "Don't worry," I said, "I got it."

"Me too," said Ari, pulling the Terwilliger Spoon out of his pocket too. "I snuck into the library."

I looked at Ari. Ari looked at me. Without thinking about it – I was tired of thinking about it – we both put our spoons into the Dunn's mailbox.

"Let them figure it out," I said and we biked away.

Chapter 11

I learned a lesson from the disaster of the Terwilliger Spoon. In fact, I learned a few lessons. First, Ari is hopeless. Why did he think he had a chance with Amanda? Amanda was hanging out with a kid three years older than her who confused muscles with personality. And what does that say about Amanda? She'd ditch Roger for a cardboard cutout of a guy with more muscles and it'd take her two weeks to find out that he wasn't real.

Second, I learned that this is just a plain stupid way to spend my money. Thanks to the three thousand dollars I spent, there now existed a perfect copy of a really ugly spoon. Ari wasn't happier. I wasn't happier. The world wasn't happier. There had to be a better way to use the money I'd been given.

Third, I learned that working in a restaurant is really hard.

• • •

I was lying in bed the next Saturday, thinking happily about all the things I could buy and then thinking unhappily about how I couldn't buy them without lying to my parents. A new guitar? I'd been through that. A Segway scooter? Where would I keep it and where would I ride it? Expensive old baseball cards? My parents would probably never find out, but I don't care about expensive old baseball cards. A riding lawn mower? A swimming pool? A pony? Diamond cufflinks? I don't have even cuffs.

The phone rang.

"It's for you," my mother yelled up the stairs.

"Hello, Ari," I said since he's the only one who would call me that early on a Saturday morning.

"It's not Ari," said the voice.

"Mimi!"

"Yes, it's your forgotten pal, Mimi."

"Oh, I'm sorry. I was going to come over and see you today. Really. I've been wrapped up with Ari."

"How'd that go."

"It went. It's gone. It was stupid."

"Can I come over?"

"Now?"

"Yeah. Right now."

"You don't sound so good."

"Can I come over?" she insisted.

"Sure. I'll get dressed and everything."

"See you."

It took Mimi less than five minutes to get here, a new record. I met her downstairs and we went to the swing set in my backyard. I'm too big for it, but that's sort of why I like it. I feel my real age in it.

"Why the rush?" I asked as Mimi pumped her legs and got some height on the swings.

"I just wanted to get out of my house."

"What's going on?"

"Nothing."

I knew that wasn't true.

Mimi let go of the swing at its highest, sailed through the air, and landed on our lawn. That was going to leave a nasty grass stain on her butt.

"So, what do you want to do?" I asked.

"My mom and dad are fighting," she said.

"That stinks. What about?"

"My mom wants to get a job and my dad doesn't want her to."

"I thought your mom works at the Sunny Day Care Center."

"She does. Part time."

"That name always bothered me," I said, stupidly interrupting Mimi's flow. "I mean, is it a sunny day for the care center or is it sunny at the day care center? Shouldn't it really be the Sunny Day Day-Care Center?"

"Anyway," Mimi said with a point on it.

"Anyway," I said, acknowledging that I'm an idiot.

"She's been working there four days a week for a few hours while I'm at a school, but now Betty Freed's mom wants to hire my mom to work in her office. As an office manager."

"So, what's the problem?"

"It's freaked my dad out. He says it's really just a fancy name for a secretary and that my mom wouldn't like it as much as working at the day care and she'd just be doing it for the money."

"So why does your mom want to do it?"

"I think because we need the money. That's the part that's freaking me out. I think my dad's worried about getting fired. He's had that job forever."

"He works at Dunn Industries, doesn't he?" I asked. I never really paid too much attention to what jobs my friends' parents had. After all, when you hear the parents talking about work, they're almost always complaining about people you've never met. My dad's different, but that's because he's a newspaper editor which means he covers interesting things. Or maybe it's just because he's my dad.

"Yeah. He's a manager now. But he sounds like he thinks the company's going to be firing a whole bunch of people."

"That would stink." Dunn Industries was the biggest company in town. I was never sure exactly what they made, but whatever it was, it took a big factory. My father once explained that Dunn Industries makes parts for other factories: machines that build other machines. I of course immediately started to wonder who makes Dunn Industries' machines, which would be machines that build other machines for other machines. And then who made those machines? And so on until you found the factory that makes the machines that make all the other machines for building factories. That's where I'd want to work.

"Hey," I said, "Want to go to the skateboard park?"

"Yeah!" said Mimi. "Oh," she added, the light going out of

her eyes, "I don't think I can."

"Why not?"

"I'm supposed to be watching my money." It cost $4 to skateboard for an hour.

"No problem. I think I've got some extra," I said.

Off we went, talking about everything except Mimi's parents.

• • •

"What's going on with Dunn Industries?" I asked my Dad as we sat in the living room before dinner.

"What do you mean?"

"I heard they're going to fire a bunch of people."

"A layoff?"

"I don't know. What's a layoff?"

"When a company fires a bunch of people," Dad said, looking up from his magazine. "Well, that's interesting."

"Wouldn't that be bad for the town?"

"It sure wouldn't be good. Dunn employs about fifteen percent of the people in this town. If the factory has a layoff, there'll be a lot of people who have no salary any more. And there aren't that many open jobs for people to get here."

"So what do people do?"

"They get unemployment insurance for a few months to carry them over. But, ultimately, people either find a job or they have to move somewhere else."

"That's bad."

"It's bad for everyone. It's bad for the people. And it's bad for the town. When a town gets smaller, there are fewer people paying taxes, so the town has less money to spend and so it has to cut back on programs also. There's less money for schools, for parks, for the library, to fix the roads..."

We sat for a moment, thinking about what we might lose. I was thinking mainly about Mimi. I would hate it if she moved. It would change the town so much for me that it would be like *we* moved.

"Where'd you hear about this?" Dad asked.

"I don't know."

"It must have been somewhere."

"I don't feel right about telling you. The person who told me didn't say it was ok to tell anyone, especially the editor of the local paper."

"Protecting your sources? That's the first thing a good newspaper person learns to do. But I'm going to look into it."

I must have looked worried.

"Don't worry. I won't let anyone know I heard the rumor from you."

• • •

Although I couldn't buy anything my parents would notice, there were ways of spending money that they wouldn't know about. For example, I now got dessert almost every day at lunch. And my tropical fish tank was getting crowded with new citizens, including three I nicknamed "Secret," "Lee" and "Rich."

That afternoon, I had gone to the games store and bought a couple of new video games. I paid cash, of course. And even though the amount it cost me was less than my money earned in ten minutes by just sitting in the bank, it seemed wrong. I could afford it, but it still felt like a waste. I almost walked out of the store without buying anything when I decided that having $100,000,000 and being too chicken-hearted to buy even a stupid video game or two was an even bigger waste. So, I bought them and went to Ari's to play them. "That's a new game," Ari's mother said, surprising me. I don't think my parents know what games I have.

"It's Jake's," said Ari, perfectly truthfully.

It turned out that both games were actually pretty dumb, unless you can find yourself surprised when the same troll jumps out from behind the same rock every time you're forced to re-start a level, or if your idea of fun is moving down a mountain on jet-powered skis that tend to crash into trees no matter how carefully you steer them. I left the games with Ari and headed home.

It was a Friday night and it seemed as if the entire town was relaxed and looking forward to the weekend. The sky was turning that deep shade of blue that is the color I see in my mind right before I fall asleep. There was enough of a breeze to make soup a possibility but not enough to slow down my bike. I'm not one to notice the weather much, but that night was an exception.

Because it was a Friday, my father was home with a copy of his newspaper. He had been "on press" all day and seemed tired but not annoyed. I glanced at the headline and nearly blew my bubblegum out my nose: "Dunn Industries Threatens Lay Offs."

"Dad," I said, "How could you?"

"How could I what, Jake?" he said like someone who was looking forward to relaxing only to face accusations from his son. Which is exactly what he was.

"I told you about the Dunn Industry lay offs in private."

"Yes, you did. And I respected that."

"How can you say that? Look at this headline!"

"Now, Jake, I didn't use anything you told me. I went out and gathered my own information. And it confirmed the rumor you'd told me."

"What information? How did you find out?"

"I can't tell you that because then I'd be revealing *my* sources and I can't do that just like you didn't reveal your source. But, I called some people I know at Dunn Industries, and they talked to me off the record."

"What's that mean?" I asked as if there couldn't be any possible sense to such a stupid phrase. I was so angry that I was willing to set myself up to look really dumb.

"That means that they agreed to talk with me only if I promised not to reveal who they are. And I won't. But they're good sources and I think the story is true. And I think you did a good thing telling me about it. It's good for the town to know what Dunn is up to."

I didn't feel good about it. And I didn't feel any better about it on Saturday when Mimi called to tell me that her father had been fired.

Chapter 12

"That's terrible," I said to Mimi.

"So why'd you do it?" she said in a voice that was angry after crying.

"Do what?"

"Tell your father. Do you know how bad this is?"

"I didn't tell him. Not exactly. Can I come over?"

"It's not a good time. My parents are really, really upset."

"Would you meet me outside? Just for a few minutes? I'd really like to talk with you." I felt like this was more for me than for her.

"Fine," she said. "Meet me by the gnome." For the first few years I'd thought the plaster gnome in her yard was scary. Then I thought it was cute. Now I thought it was ridiculous. But this didn't seem the time to bring it up with Mimi.

I raced there on my bike. As I was hopping off, she was coming out her front door.

"So?" she asked the way someone points a finger at a dog that's been bad.

"So, I did tell my father."

"How could you?"

"But I told him confidentially. He didn't use what I told him. He went out and found other people to talk with."

"What other people?"

I picked up some of the gravel around the gnome and threw it at the big oak tree in the middle of Mimi's yard.

"Don't do that," she said. Her parents didn't like it. Somehow, I was reassured by her criticizing me this way.

"He wouldn't tell me because those sources were confidential also."

"Well, Mr. Dunn is convinced it was my father who told."

"Why?"

"I don't know. My parents are so upset that they're not making a lot of sense. Mr. Dunn only told a few people. My father was one of them."

"We should tell Mr. Dunn it didn't come from your father. My father will tell him."

"It wouldn't matter. Dad's already given up."

"Well, that's dumb," I said. Mimi shot me a look as if I'd just said that her father was dumb. "No, not dumb dumb," I explained. "Just, like, well, he should keep trying. I bet my father can get him his job back."

"Would he tell Mr. Dunn who his source was?" I shook my head. "So what good would it do?"

Someone was mowing a lawn as the sun went down.

"I don't know what's going to happen," said Mimi finally. "What do you do when your father is out of work and your mother works part time? How do you have enough money for food, and a car, and heating?"

"My dad says you get uninsurance employment."

"Unemployment insurance," Mimi corrected. "But I don't think that lasts very long." We could hear plates being rattled in Mimi's house as they were put away from dinner. "I guess Mom will take that job after all."

"I guess."

I sat next to my friend Mimi, waiting for her to cry. She didn't.

• • •

My dad was reading a biography of Winston Churchill, the British wartime leader who said so many witty things that every ten minutes Dad would chuckle and read us something from the book. Apparently, Churchill also had a terrible British accent. My mother was knitting. The clack of her needles was like the sound of a fast typist. She is a knitting demon. "That's how I got through grad school courses," she liked to say. Maddie was playing a game of solitaire using a deck with pictures of witches, ogres, fairies and the occasional frog wearing a prince's crown. I like it when she plays solitaire because then she's not asking me to play.

"Want to play?" Maddie asked me.

"I thought you were playing solitaire."

"I am but there's a way to play two-person."

"Maybe later," I said. By "later" I meant "When the sun is flickering out because it's run out of fuel and the universe has collapsed into a dot the size of your brain."

I was too busy thinking about what Mimi had asked: "What do you do when your father is out of work and your mother works part time?" I realized now that that was the wrong question. The right one is: "What do you do when your father is out of work and your mother works part time and you have a friend who has $100 million in the bank?"

• • •

I was supposed to hang out with Ari on Saturday, but I called him and said that I needed to spend some quality time with Mimi. He's a good enough friend that he didn't act all hurt and make me feel bad about it. "Do you want me to come with you?" he asked.

"No, I think it'll be better if it's just me," I said.

It was a beautiful, sunny Saturday. There weren't any flowers yet, but you could smell the earth getting ready. I walked through out small front yard and saw the two weekly local papers stacked next to one another on a chair on our porch. I took them to the swing. The headline in *The Gaz* was "Dunn Industries Denies Report It Is to Lay Off Dozens." There was a picture of Mr. Dunn denying the report, looking rather splendid in his suit and perfect hair. The other headlines reported on a drop in the testing scores at the high school, a local author whose book won an award, and a controversy over one of the gas stations whose gasoline fumes were disturbing the neighbors.

The Boynton County Register, Mr. Dunn's paper, had a very different set of headlines:

Mama Mia, That's a Pizza!
(A local pizza parlor makes a very big pizza)

Look Out Dragons, the Knights Are On The Way!

(The high school swim team is going to take on another school's team.)

How Much Are Those Doggies in the Window?

(A new pet store has opened and has some cute puppies for sale.)

Little Orphan Frannie Stars!

(The local theater group is putting on "Little Orphan Annie" starring Frannie Moss. I go to school with Frannie and hate her.)

Eat Your Way to Slim!

(A diet clinic in town is having a sale.)

Up on the Roof!

(Mr. Emmet Birdsall was cleaning his roof's gutters when *The Register's* photographer happened by.)

If I had to explain my problem with *The Register* in a sentence, it'd be: too many exclamation points, not enough news. I couldn't read *The Register* without becoming more proud of my father. *The Gaz* was so much better. I put both newspapers on the porch and walked to Mimi's house.

When Mimi answered my knock on the door, she did the opposite of inviting me in. She stepped outside, even though she didn't have shoes on, and made it clear that she didn't want me going in. Through the kitchen window I could see her father in a bathrobe. He didn't look happy and I guessed that seeing the son of the editor who got him fired wouldn't have made him any happier. Seeing her father made me especially appreciate Mimi's willingness to hang out with me.

"How's it going?" I asked, stupidly.

"You know. The same," Mimi answered.

"I was wondering if you wanted to sell choco-bricks."

"I dunno. Yeah, maybe."

Choco-bricks were small fake bricks made of chocolate that we were supposed to be selling to raise money for the school extension program. Our middle school was getting too small – or, "Kids Are Bustin' Out!" as *The Register* might put it – so we were sent out to raise money. I wondered how much the company that made the crummy Choco-bricks and the donation cards and all the rest of it made out of us poor student slaves who were supposed to be happy spending our Saturday selling candy that no one wants just so we can earn our little flashlight or compass, depending on how far up the "Choco-Brick Super Sales Pyramid" we went.

But it beat moping.

So, Mimi went into her house and got her Choco-Brick-o-Kit, biked to my house where I grabbed mine, and we headed over to the U-Do-It parking lot thinking that people spending money on household renovations would probably feel guilty about turning down two cute kids like me and Mimi. Well, Mimi's cute. I'm handsome in a rugged way. (Yeah, right.)

Did you ever want to be invisible? Then come to the

parking lot at the U-Do-It lot with a bunch of Choco-bricks to sell. People wheeled their carts through the lot as if their shoes were about to burst into flame. And they were big carts, designed to fit wall panels, beams big enough to hold up a living room, and even an entire fireplace that looked real on the outside but on the inside was made of the same plastic as Maddie's backyard slide. And it turns out that people who have just bought wall panels, living room beams, and fake fireplaces are too focused on getting home and getting to work to buy lousy candy from two extremely cute eighth graders.

We tried every trick in the book:

o *The Standard Approach*: We go up to a stranger and say in a cheerful voice, "Hi! We're selling bricks of chocolate to help raise money for real bricks so we can build new classrooms for our school. They're only $5 and ..." That's about as far as we got with most people.

o *The Pity Approach*: We look at the ground and shuffle our feet while trying to catch the eye of a shopper. "We're having a lot of trouble raising money for our school. There just isn't enough room..." Mimi was better at this than me, maybe because when I try to act sad it comes out as being angry.

o *The Entertainment Approach*: Mimi says, "We're selling bricks..." and I pretend to interrupt with "But they're not real bricks..." and then she says, "You can eat these bricks..." and I say, "Eat bricks? How can that be, Mimi." And she says, "These are chocolate bricks, Jake! Deee-licious!" And I say, "I bet it's for a good

110

cause." And she says, "And how…" and that's about when the shopper would turn away like a person changing the dial on an obnoxious TV show.

o *The Honest Approach*: We walk up quickly to a shopper. Mimi stands on the left and I stand on the right so they have no way to escape except by backing up which is hard to do if you have a cart filled with wall panels and fake fireplaces. "We're raising money for our school," Mimi says. "We're selling these blocks of chocolate," I say. "They taste bad and they're over-priced, but it's for a really good cause." That was our most effective technique. With it, we sold close to four choco-bricks in an hour, if you count two as being close to four.

Mimi and I sat on the curb and counted our receipts. One two. Then we double checked. One two. We added up the money we had made. Ten dollars.

"You know," I said, "this is ridiculous."

"You mean trying to sell chocolate bricks to people who are buying ant poison for their house?"

"You know what I mean. I figured out how much interest I make."

"You mean like the interest I make every year on my bank account?"

"Yeah. What do you make in a year?"

"Last year I made about four dollars."

"I make $16,438."

"Wow! You get that in a year for doing nothing?"

"No, sorry, Mimi. That's how much interest I make every day."

"A day??" She was practically shouting.

"Yup."

"That's $600 an hour!"

"Actually, it's almost $700 an hour."

"Oh my gosh, Jake. You're rich!"

"Weird, isn't it? And could you keep it down a little?" A couple carrying bags full of electrical parts had turned to look. I'm sure they thought I'd found fifty cents on the ground or something. "I am seriously rich," I said to Mimi.

"So, what are we doing standing here selling stupid Choco-bricks to people who don't want them?"

"Having fun?"

"You wish," she said. "How much do you think the entire school earns from selling stupid Choco-bricks?" We'd grown to think of "stupid Choco-bricks" as one word.

"I think we made $1,500 or so last year. And that was a good year."

"Jake, you make that in two hours doing nothing. Why have we been standing out here making fools of ourselves?"

"And most of that $1,500 goes to the Choco-brick company, I'm sure." I said. "We'd be better off just giving it straight to the school."

Mimi flipped the brim of her hat up. "I am now out of the stupid Choco-brick business for good." She looked at me.

"Depending, of course, on how generous you're feeling."

"How many Choco-bricks do you want to have sold?"

"A hundred?"

"No one will believe a hundred."

"Ok, fifty."

"That'd make you the class leader."

"I'm ok with that."

"It worries me a little. How about 45?"

"Ok. And how many are you going to sell yourself?"

"I'm not greedy. How about 35?"

"Make it 38. I don't want to beat you by that much."

"What do we do with the chocolate?" Mimi asked.

"What do you mean?"

"Well, you're about to buy 44 bars from me. What do I do with 44 bars of chocolate?"

"First, we eat one." I took two from my box and handed one to Mimi. We unwrapped the bars halfway and held them carefully. The chocolate was limp from having sat in the sun. We ate quickly. They were bad. And for this we were overcharging people?

I held up my half-finished bar. "I am done. I'm more than done. I'm overdone."

Mimi held hers upside down and watched the gooey chocolate run onto the edge of the parking lot. "Yuch. For this we're overcharging people?" (Mimi had the habit of saying

113

what I was thinking.)

We stood up with the boxes of bars under our arms. As we got on our bikes, we saw a familiar boy bicycling up.

"Hey," said Ari, "How's the fishing here? Sold many?"

"I sold 45," said Mimi.

"I sold 38," I said.

"Wow!" said Ari. "This must be the best spot in the entire town!"

"Yeah," I said, "But you have to have the right technique."

"Yeah," said Mimi. "We had no luck until we talked in a French accent," she explained, demonstrating her technique. Mimi's French accent sounded like a cartoon mouse.

"Zat's right," I said in my own unique French. "Ze custom-airs zeem to lahk it bettah if zey t'ink you har an exchahnge 'tudent."

"Wow!" said Ari again. "Thanks!"

I was all for watching him try it but Mimi didn't have the heart and told him the truth. Ari sold 39 boxes that afternoon, and it only took him about fifteen seconds. With no French accent.

Chapter 13

I didn't feel good about dreading Helpful Citizen day. But that's the truth: I definitely wasn't looking forward to it. Oakes School thinks, "No education is complete without service." Or, as the t-shirts said, "Helpful Citizen Day: Learning to give a helping hand." There was a picture of a big hand reaching down to take a little hand, drawn in a childish way, which would have been better if a child had actually drawn it. Whenever I see grownup pictures drawn to look like children did them, with stick figures and houses that have their perspective all wrong, I feel like they're making fun of us. We're just kids. We would draw better if we could.

But the drawing wasn't what bothered me about the day. I have nothing against doing volunteer work. For example, I participate in the Keep Us Green day, planting flowers along the roads. And I sort recyclables a couple times a year down at the dump. That's fun, especially the part where you get to throw the glass bottles into the big hopper and watch them break. But being forced to volunteer makes as much sense to me as being forced to play. It's not play if you're forced, and it's not volunteering if you have no choice about it.

To make it worse, I was put in the group going to the Senior Recreational Center attached to Dunn Village, a block of apartments Mr. Dunn rented mainly to old people. I don't know what to say to old people, unless I know them, like my grandparents or Mrs. Fordgythe. Meeting anyone for the first time and having to have a "pleasant chat" is just hard for me. And, judging from Ari and Mimi's reactions, hard for them, too.

At least we'd all been assigned to the same group. On the other hand, I would rather have been assigned to the group painting the fence at the park or the group doing the gardening at the long-term care section of the hospital. I did manage to get out of the petting zoo job. All the other students thought it was the best of all the volunteer offerings, but I'd heard from a good source (my older cousin Max) that instead of hanging around the cute ponies and lambs the way you imagine, you have to shovel stuff. Say no more. So when the kids who were assigned to the zoo found out about it and pumped their fists and said "Yes!" it was all I could do not to laugh.

There were six of us in the Senior Center group, led by the too-perky Ms. Floyd, our math teacher. I used to think that Ms. Floyd was cheery on purpose to counter the bad mood of her students since most students don't like math class. It's like a dentist who knows that she's about to hurt you so she talks in a high-pitched voice and smiles as she says, "This may hurty-wurty just an eensy-weensy bit." The higher the voice and the younger the baby talk, the more trouble you're in. Helpful Citizen Day changed my mind about Ms. Floyd. But I don't want to get ahead of myself.

I realized that the day was not going to go quite as smoothly as planned as we were unloading the minivan that brought us. We pulled up into the semi-circular driveway and even before the van stopped, three senior citizens – actually, do you mind if I just call them "old people" from now on? – were coming out the door to great us. One was the organizer, Mrs. Muldauer. Behind her were an old man and an old woman. They all seemed so glad to see us. All the kids went around to the back of the van as Ms. Floyd used both hands to shake Mrs. Muldauer's hand, leaning in, smiling even more broadly than usual. As Mrs. Muldauer introduced her two companions, we were pulling easels out of the van. When I say "we," I mean Mimi, Ari and me along with Halley Jackson, a girl who was always always always enthusiastic. When I say "we," I definitely do not mean Amanda and Lydia who were less happy about being in our group than we were to have them. They stood near enough to the door of the van to look like maybe they were about to do something without actually doing anything.

That's fine. (Well, not really.) There wasn't all that much to carry. What wasn't fine was when Mrs. Muldauer came up to us to greet us. She introduced her companions as Bill Tidewater and Felicia Markson. We all said hello to Mr. Tidewater and Ms. Markson, except for Amanda who made a point of referring to them as Bill and Felicity. Even if Amanda had gotten Ms. Markson's first name right, it wouldn't have been fine.

But here's the real giveaway. When Mr. Tidewater said, "Can I give you a hand?" Amanda said "Yeah," and handed him some poster board signs to carry.

Definitely not fine.

Halley stepped in before anyone else could and said, "Oh, thanks for offering, but I can grab those." Halley was already carrying two boxes of games and a grocery bag with cookies, but that didn't stop her. Amanda went right ahead and handed Halley the poster boards. "Thanks," said Halley. "Thanks so much."

Throughout this entire interaction, Ari stood there, studying Amanda like a boy taking an eye exam.

The Senior Center looked on the outside like a mansion. The front porch had marble pillars, and ivy had grown up the walls. But, when I brushed against one of the pillars I discovered that they were wood painted to look like marble. And the brick walls behind the ivy were stained black from soot, except where they were crumbling, revealing fresher orange brick inside.

The front entrance opened into a large room with a linoleum floor that was scuffed and dirty, and even sagged in spots. Long cafeteria tables were spread out, some with plastic tablecloths. No two table cloths matched. In fact, one looked exactly like the shower curtain in our upstairs bathroom at home. Off to the left and to the right were smaller rooms for various activities, including one with game boards set up for chess and checkers, one with a small TV placed in a piece of furniture designed for a much larger set, and a room with a couple of computers in it. Ari and I looked at one another. We knew where we'd be going first.

But I was interested in the layout of the building for another reason. I had brought with me an ordinary looking envelope. It was surprising how small a stack $10,000 can make when you get it in thousand dollar bills.

Ms. Floyd gathered us together and said, "Why don't you all just make yourselves at home here for the first hour or so? Meet the people, make some new friends, and then let's get back together at 10:15 sharp. See that clock on the wall?" It was an ancient dial clock, not in the "beautiful and old" sense but in the "scratched and should have been replaced ten years ago" sense. "So you all be punctual."

Mimi moved immediately to a table in the main room where a woman was looking through a photo album. Ari and I headed for the computer room. There were two old people in it. Neither was using a computer. And we could see why. The computers were ancient in the "did they ever really make computers this bad?" sense. The screens only showed 16 colors. The machines had 5.25" floppy drives, which meant that the only software they could run had to have been made fifteen years ago. And the only connection these machines had ever had to a web was one left by a spider.

Ari and I had been hoping that the computers would give us an easy way to talk with the old guys. We could show them some of our favorite Web sites, teach them how to play checkers on line, introduce them to the idea of mailing lists that talk about whatever it is that old people like to talk about. Now the easy path of discussion was closed off. I swallowed, turned to the old person nearest me, and started a conversation the hard way.

"Hello," I said. "My name is Jake. "

"Hello, Jake. I'm Thomas Sadler. It's a pleasure to meet you," was the reply. So, the direct approach worked. In fact, it worked a lot better than Ari's approach. I heard him say, "Hey, well, hey." Fortunately, the man he was addressing was better at this than Ari. "Hello," said the man, "My name is Frederick Hallstadt. I see you like computers…"

Mr. Sadler and I talked about the book he was reading. It

was a western, not a type of novel I particularly cared for. I prefer books with swords, magic and chain mail. But it turned out that Mr. Sadler read cowboy novels because he liked to see how wrong they were. He had been a cowboy for a few years when he was a young man. And to answer your question before you ask it: No, he didn't strap a six-shooter onto his leg and have shoot-outs with bad guys in black hats. "Sometimes they wore gray hats or white hats, or even once an orange golf hat," Mr. Sadler said. "Just kidding," he added. Mr. Sadler, dressed in a faded checked shirt, did look a little like an old cowboy. Only one thing was out of place for an old cowboy: a handkerchief neatly folded in his shirt's breast pocket.

Although Mr. Sadler was in the computer room because he could talk with his friend Mr. Hallstadt without disturbing anyone else, he was interested in computers. He asked me a lot of questions about the Internet. He had a grandson across the country who wanted to send him email, and some of his old friends in different parts of the country had told him that they were staying in touch through instant messaging. And he wanted to know if our congresswoman answered email because he was very upset about the cutbacks in funding for education. I thanked him.

Before I knew it, the ancient clock in the other room, which I could see through the doorway, said that our hour was up. I got up and interrupted Ari to let him know. Actually, I interrupted Mr. Hallstadt. Apparently Ari had managed to get him really irritated; from what I could overhear, it had something to do with Ari's tendency to say, "Well, if you say so," whenever he didn't have an opinion on a topic.

Predictably, Amanda and Lydia kept us waiting. The rest of us sat at the table with my family's shower curtain on it, chatting about the people we met. Mimi had talked with a group of three women who had known one another for over sixty years, two of whom had disliked each other for over fifty years. The morning light came through a set of large windows on the far wall. A string of letters that spelled out "Happy Birthday" was taped across the center windows, and bits of tape from decades of other signs blotched the glass here and there. But the light was strong and bright enough for me to notice the little specks of dust floating everywhere, like confetti at a parade.

Fifteen minutes later, Amanda and Lydia came in from a back door that led to the outside. I saw Lydia stuffing a little plastic bag from the Sweet Nothings clothing store into her backpack.

"You must have gotten lost talking to these wonderful people," Ms. Floyd said to Amanda and Lydia. Don't do that, I thought. Don't make up their excuses for them. At least let us see what they'd come up with. "Well, let's try to keep to our schedule, ok? And the next thing is what we're really here for: life stories." She paused, as if we were supposed to clap our hands in joy. "Everyone take a notebook and if you forgot a pen, I brought some extras." Amanda and Lydia took pens. "Now, each of you is going to find a senior and help him or her write his or her life story."

"How long does it have to be?" asked Amanda

"You'll have an hour and a half," said Ms. Floyd. Amanda rolled her eyes. "So keep track of the time to make sure you get all the way through. You're not going to write the life story now. You're just going to take notes. We'll write up the final version back at home."

Lydia said, "That's not fair." Amanda popped her bubblegum in agreement. I could read what she was thinking: Lend a Helping Hand Day wasn't supposed to include homework.

Ms. Floyd seemed to have read the same message. "Your English teachers have agreed to count this as a writing project." We had to write six projects over the course of the year. "Now, there's one more thing. I don't want this to be just 'I was born in 19-something and then we moved to wherever in 19-something-else and then I went to school.' I want you each to get one great story from each senior. One thing in their lives that makes a great story. So, you'll have notes about all the important events in their lives but you'll have one, long piece that tells this great story. Everyone understand?"

Ari asked, "So the rest of it should just be dates and places?"

"No," said Ms. Floyd, "but it's a good question." No, it wasn't. "You should write the whole biography as if it were story, not just places and dates. We want these Life Stories to tell the truth about their lives in a way that the seniors themselves would recognize. Ok? Then let's go. We'll meet back here in an hour and a half. Oh, and we'll be reading the stories at the cupcake social after lunch."

Ari and I went back into the computer room where Mr. Sadler and Mr. Halstadt were talking. Ari whispered to me, "Can we both do one guy?" I shook my head and sat next to

Mr. Sadler. Through the door, I could see Ms. Floyd hustling Amanda and Lydia along. Now she was shaking her head and telling the girls to go in different directions; apparently, they, like Ari, were hoping to double-team an old person.

"Mr. Sadler," I said, "I'd like to write up your autobiography."

"Me?" he asked in surprise, adjusting the handkerchief in his pocked. "I haven't done anything worth writing up."

"Oh, I'm sure that's not true," I said, having no idea if that was true or not. "Besides, we only have an hour and a half to take notes. Then I'll write it up after we leave. So, it will really be just a quick overview. But, I need to have one really good story. We're going to read them after our little party here this afternoon."

"One good story? I don't know. I can't think of any."

"Why don't we just start from the beginning and get down the basics of your life? And we can worry about the story afterwards."

"There's not much to tell..."

Hah!

Mr. Sadler – Thomas Beecham Sadler – was born in 1917. "I was raised by my grandparents after my father died when I was three. Grandma and Grandpa moved in and my mother never really got her bearings back. Grandma and Grandpa were wonderful folks. Grandma taught herself to read when she was a child, and when she met Grandpa when he was fifteen, she taught him how to read, too." He paused to let me catch up with my note taking, adding casually, "They were born slaves, you know."

The words didn't hit me until a few seconds after he said them. "Slaves?" I asked. It didn't seem possible that in the 21st century I could be talking to someone who actually knew slaves. But I did the math mentally. They could have been five or even ten years old at the end of the Civil War. "That's amazing."

"Yes it is. In fact, you see how I wear a handkerchief like this in my breast pocket? That's because my grandpa taught me that a gentleman always has a handkerchief neatly folded and ready. And I've always believed that he picked that up from his master. So, you're seeing a slave master's manners displayed in the grandson of a slave. I do it on purpose. It's a reminder."

"In fact," Mr. Sadler said, "it played a part in the story of how I met one of the richest men in the West." And then Mr. Sadler told me the story...

• • •

It was the worst of the Great Depression. Mr. Sadler – or Beech, as he was known then – was a teen-ager in Chicago. His family had already been on the edge of poverty. Now the great waves of unemployment pushed them over the edge. Before, everyone in the family, including the children, had to work to bring in enough money for food, but now there just wasn't any work. When Beech's father got laid off, the family decided that Beech, as the eldest, should go where the jobs were. So, Beech headed out west. He was sixteen, had a few dollars in his pocket, not much more than the clothes he was wearing, and no idea of where he would go. His only two comforts were that his best friend, Dill "Pink" McDaniels was with him, and he had his grandfather's handkerchief neatly folded in his breast pocket.

So the two boys walked, hitched, and rode the rails until they got to Montana. That's just where the road led them. In Durbin, a small town dominated by a very large ranch, they saw a sign in the local feed shop's window. "Cowboys wanted." Beech looked at Pink. Pink looked at Beech. They laughed. They had been turned down for so many jobs that the idea of becoming African-American cowboys was just ridiculous. All he and Pink knew about cowboys they had learned from the movies: ropin' and shootin' and gettin' the purty girl at the end.

So, there they stood in the main street of tiny Durbin, pretending to draw on each other and laughing, when a large white man said, "What are you boys laughing at?" Beech looked at him. He was wore an expensive blue suit, solid gold cufflinks, a ring on his finger with a green jewel the size of a small potato ... and a cowboy belt, cowboy hat, and cowboy boots.

"Nothing, sir," said Beech, looking down at the ground as was proper at that time.

"Well, something obviously is entertaining you two boys. You should let us in on the joke." The man gestured to three other men, smaller than him and not as expensively dressed, who stood behind him. "So, what is so goldurned funny?"

"We were just laughing at the idea of us applying for the cowboy job."

"And what's so funny about that?"

"Well, sir, we're Negroes."

"I can see that. You don't know much about cowboys, do you?"

"No sir."

"Just what you've seen in the movies."

"Yes sir."

"The fact is that there have been plenty of Negro cowboys. Isn't that right, Sam?" he asked the man closest to him. Sam looked puzzled. "Sam doesn't know anything either. But there have been. Ain't nothing funny about it."

"Yes sir."

"Do you boys want to be cowboys?"

Beech and Pink looked at one another, not knowing what the right answer was supposed to be. "We want to work," said Beech.

"Then you are the two luckiest black boys this side of the Mississippi," he said, although he used a much worse word for "black boys." "I'm C. Carter Hargreaves, the owner of the largest ranch in Montana and the richest man you'll ever meet, and I'm going to hire you. I'll tell you why. Out here, we don't care what the color of your skin is. What matters is how hard you want to work. Sam, go sign these boys up and take 'em out to the Slanted Pine."

"Thank you, sir!" they both said more than once.

"Don't thank me. Theo out at the ranch will work you

hard. If you can't keep up, then, well, we'll let you go and no hard feelings." He turned to leave but then asked one more question: "You boys know how to ride? No? Theo will teach you." He laughed again.

And Beech and Pink did work hard. For two years. They started with which end of the cow to milk and moved to riding, roping, and how live outside for weeks at a time. Theo was a good teacher, but not a kind one. You paid for your mistakes in aches and pains at best, and with bruises and deductions from your pay at worst.

During all this time, they saw C. Carter Hargreaves on rare occasion, usually at a great distance, standing on the porch of his huge house, hands on his hips, smoking a cigar. Whenever they got close enough to him to be noticed, he'd tip his hat at them in acknowledgement, and once he asked them how Theo was treating them.

Over time, Pink and Beech realized that despite what Mr. Hargreaves had said, they were the only black cowboys working at the Slanted Pine. They became better friends than ever, relying on each other for help and encouragement…. until one day, the two of them were walking down the main street on their day off. Out of the bank strode Mr. Hargreaves, summery in a white suit and a straw hat. "Howdy, boys," he said, and then, to their surprise turned in his tracks and approached them. He leaned in towards Beech and said, "Can I have a word with you?"

They walked across the street, leaving Pink to try to figure out what they were talking about. "I've had my eye on you," said Mr. Hargreaves.

Beech didn't know if this was a good thing or a bad thing. "I've been impressed with what you've learned. I'd like you to be Theo's second trail hand." This would give Beech more responsibility and just a little more pay.

"Well, that would be fine," said Beech. "Thank you, sir."

"No, no, you've earned it."

Becoming second trail hand meant that Beech got up earlier and worked later than ever before. But he noticed that Pink seemed hurt. "Come ride next to me," Beech said one day, waving his friend forward. As they rode along the edge of the herd of cattle, Pink confessed that he was bothered by the extra 25 cents a week Beech was getting. "The money doesn't mean anything," said Beech. And, after talking some more, it turned that what really stung Pink was what the raise meant: Mr. Hargreaves favored Beech. "You ride better than I do and you rope a whole lot better," Beech told his friend. "Who knows why he picked me instead of you. Just luck." It didn't take long for these true friends to smooth out the kink.

Just two weeks later Pink had a chance to prove that he was the better cowboy. That night Theo had produced a couple of bottles of whiskey he'd packed. The little group of cowboys on the trail proceeded to get so drunk that one of them fell asleep on a rattlesnake which was so surprised that it slithered away without biting. Beech and Pink were the only ones left sober because the bottle had been passed from white hand to white hand. Besides, Beech was never one for drinking.

The stars were out and the moon was below the horizon. Beech was lying on his back almost asleep when a gun went off next to him. He and Pink bolted upright, but the other cowboys had barely stirred. They saw a smoking gun in the hand of Fred Barker, an older cowhand who had fallen asleep holding it, and fired it in his sleep without even waking himself up.

But the cattle had noticed. Four hundred cows were moving. Beech and Pink tried to wake Theo but he just rolled over in the middle of a snore. "No time," said Beech, jumping into the saddle. He and Pink went off at full gallop to prevent the cows from stampeding.

The sound of 400 cows moving together isn't something you hear. You feel it. The ground becomes a trampoline, pushing up against you and suddenly dropping beneath you. "They're headed for the cliff!" yelled Beech, spurring his horse with Pink close behind.

Cattle are stupid but not stupid enough to jump off a cliff. But if they stampede alongside of one, the ones on the edge can be pushed over the side because of the sheer rampaging mass of flesh that's moving without plan or sense. Pink galloped ahead of Beech, putting his horse between the cliff and the cattle, herding them away from danger. He controlled his horse with a precision and confidence that awed Beech. And the cattle were turning towards safety.

Just as Beech thought they were over the worst of it, he saw Pink's horse go down. A panicked cow had moved the wrong way and the horse lost its footing along the side of the cliff. The horse started to right itself, but Pink was nowhere to be seen. Beech pulled ahead and jumped off his horse. Peering over the side, sick with worry, he saw his friend balanced on an incline too steep to climb and too high to roll down. It didn't take any fancy rope twirling to get a line to his friend, and Pink quickly clambered up to safety. Then they both began to laugh, although neither could tell you why. And then they brought the herd of cattle back to where the other cowboys were still sleeping, all except for Theo who nodded at them once, pulled the brim of his hat over his eyes, and went back to sleep.

The next day, as they were riding slowly and the sun was down low enough that the air had already begun to cool, Beech asked Pink, "Why do we do it?"

"Do what?"

"Ride horses next to cliffs to protect cattle."

"Because it's our job."

"We didn't risk our lives because it's our job. Our lives aren't worth a couple of lost cattle."

"But that's not up to us to decide. They're Mr. Hargreaves' cows. We owe him for hiring us."

"You're right, Pink. He hired us even though we're the darkest faced cowboys we've met so far. That counts for something."

"Here's to Mr. Hargreaves," said Pink, toasting him with his canteen.

Three weeks later, the crew came back to town. Beech and Pink had a bath at the wash house, aired out their bedding, and collected their pay. They'd been back for three days when Beech got a ride into town to get his saddle fixed. As he was coming out of the leather repair shop, he saw Mr. Hargreaves walking towards him. Beech took off his hat and nodded a greeting.

"I want to speak with you," said Mr. Hargreaves.

"Yes, sir."

"I hear you and your friend did a mighty brave thing a couple of weeks back."

"We just did what we were hired to do."

"Well, you did it when the rest of the crew was dead drunk. And, I understand that you did it at the risk of grave personal danger."

"We just…"

"No, don't downplay it. I want you and everyone to know that I recognize such bravery. I want you to have this as my reward." He put a bill into Beech's hand. "No, don't thank me. You earned it." He shook Beech's hand and walked on. "I have one of those for your friend as well."

In his palm was a $50 bill.

It wasn't just the money that filled Beech's heart with joy. It was the fact that he had worked hard and was being recognized for what he was and what he'd done. Of course, getting a year's salary all at once wasn't nothing! He knew what a difference the extra money would make to his family back home.

Beech ran straight back to the ranch and found Pink washing the lunch dishes behind the cookhouse. "Pink! Pink!" Beech yelled. "You won't believe what happened!" And Pink didn't believe him until Beech showed him the fifty dollar bill. "And Mr. Hargreaves says that when he sees you, you're going to get one, too."

Pink sat down on the ground, amazed. "That Mr. Hargreaves…" he began.

"I know," said Beech. "I've met a lot of white men," he said, as if he weren't just nineteen years old. "A few have been mean, and more than that have been nice, but to almost all of them I was invisible. Just another dark face like a thousand others they don't notice."

"That's the truth," said Pink. "The only time I'm noticed by a white person, it's either because I'm in the way or they expect me to do something for them. And I wouldn't even mind so much if just once they'd look me in the eyes, and maybe even ask me my name."

"Well, Mr. Hargreaves is the exception," said Beech.

"Fifty dollars!" Pink exclaimed.

"Do you reckon we can spend some on ourselves?"

"I think our parents would insist on it. What are you thinking of doing for yourself?"

"Well, I don't think we want to let our trail partners know that we've come into money. They might resent it."

"That's right. I'm not sure how it'd sit with them if they found out that the two Negro cowboys had been so well rewarded." They sat on the ground and talked about what they could buy that wouldn't make them look rich.

The next day, Beech was all for going into town to spend a little of their money. "You go," said Pink. "I'm not feeling too well." He was just plain worn out from the weeks on the trail.

So, Beech went into town by himself for the second day in a row.

After having bought a checked shirt and a new leather strap to hold his sleeping roll onto his saddle, Beech was sitting on a bench at the edge of the town square. There was nothing in the square except the trash that had blown in and a small aspen tree with only a few dozen leaves on it keeping it alive. Beech was eating a sandwich he had brought with him when he saw Mr. Hargreaves approaching.

"I want to speak with you," said Mr. Hargreaves.

"Yes, sir," said Beech. But before he could thank Mr. Hargreaves for his generosity, he was cut off.

"I hear you and your friend did a mighty brave thing a couple of weeks back," said Mr. Hargreaves.

"Well..." Beech began, confused. Hadn't they had this conversation already?

"Now, did your friend tell you about the little bonus I have for you?"

"I don't understand..."

"Well, if he's really your buddy, he should have told you. Anyway, I understand that you acted at the risk of grave personal danger."

"But..."

"No, don't downplay it. I want you and everyone to know that I recognize such bravery. I want you to have this as my reward." He put a bill into Beech's hand. "No, don't thank me. You earned it." He shook Beech's hand and walked on. "And

133

tell your friend to make sure he passes messages along to you. It's not every day that a young Negro gets a $50 bill pressed into his palm. " Except Mr. Hargreaves used a term much worse than "Negro."

Beech stepped back, not wanting to understand what had happened. Two black faces in the entire town, and Mr. Hargreaves couldn't tell them apart.

"Don't you even say Thank you?" demanded Mr. Hargreaves. "Didn't your momma teach you any manners, boy?"

Beech didn't know what to say. In nervousness, he touched the clean, white handkerchief in his breast pocket. "Thank you…" he began.

Mr. Hargreaves' eyes followed Beech's hand to the handkerchief. Beech could see the color rise in Mr. Hargreaves' face as he realized his blunder. "You're the Negro who wears a handkerchief in his pocket," he said. "I gave you money yesterday. Well, son, you can give this bill to your friend."

Mr. Hargreaves started to turn away.

"No, sir," said Beech.

"Excuse me, son? What did you say?"

"I said no, sir. No thank you. I will not give this fifty to my friend. He has a name. It's Bill McDaniels. His friends call him Pink. I will give him the fifty you gave me yesterday, but I don't want this one. Here it is back, Mr. Hargreaves, sir, with my thanks. But you don't even know who you're thanking. Me and my friend Pink have worked hard for you. And, we're no heroes but we did save a herd of your cattle by steering them away from a cliff. Yes, sir. And you owe us your thanks. But you can't thank a man unless you know who is, and you have had two years to learn our names. So, I appreciate the money, and Lord knows my family could use it, but I can't rightly take it from you."

Mr. Hargreaves looked at him solemnly. "What's your name, son?"

"It's Thomas Beecham Sadler. From the Chicago Sadlers, formerly the Georgia Sadlers, a slave family."

"Well, Thomas Beecham Sadler. I've learned something from you. So I'm going to let you keep that fifty dollars because that was a fifty dollar lesson." Beech took it back uncertainly. Mr. Hargreaves continued: "But you've also embarrassed me, son. And I haven't become who I am by being embarrassed by little Negro boys. So, take your money, pack your goods, and get off my ranch. You're fired, son."

Beech walked back to the ranch slowly, looking at the dust kicked up by the tips of his shoes. He felt oddly calm. No matter how hard he had worked and how good a job he had done, he was still only skin deep to Mr. Hargreaves. He was at best "the Negro with the handkerchief." That's not what his grandfather had hoped for on the day he was set free.

"I've been a cowboy long enough," he told Pink. "Want to come with me?"

Pink stayed. Beech left the next day and began the rest of his life.

● ● ●

I barely took notes while he was talking. But I remembered it all and began to write it up as soon as I had asked him about the rest of his life. We didn't have much time left, and I wrote quickly.

I had one more thing to do. As Ari and I stood up to head back to where Ms. Floyd was standing in the main hall, Ari created a distraction, as we had agreed. Unfortunately, Ari's idea of a distraction was to say, "Oh, look!" in an unconvincing voice and point into the main hall. When Ari again said "Oh, look!" this time louder and more obviously faking it, and when again neither Mr. Sadler nor Mr. Hallstadt even turned their heads, I just walked to a small table behind both their chairs and left the envelope. They would have had to have had eyes in the backs of their heads to see me. I had printed on the letter "For the People of Dunn Village Recreational Center" in big letters that no one could miss. I hoped.

A the little party the residents nibbled on oatmeal cookies, sipped punch, and talked about the weather, sports, and how to tan a zebra hide. (Mrs. Wilcox had apparently spent time in Africa.) When it was time to stand up and tell the stories we had gathered, I could hardly wait. But I had to.

Halley went first. She told about the time that Bill Tidewater met John F. Kennedy. Kennedy had been a young senator from Massachusetts at the time and Mr. Tidewater was working as a cab driver to supplement the income from his job as a landscape gardener. Senator Kennedy asked Mr. Tidewater why he had to work so hard, and when he replied that it was so he could get his son the medical treatment he needed to learn to walk after coming down with polio, the Senator promised to work on providing health care for working people. Maybe Mr. Tidewater changed history that day.

Then it was Ari's turn. In typical fashion, it took Ari a long time to find his topic. First he talked about where Mr. Hallstadt was born and about how his parents had come from Germany before the first World War. Then he talked about a book Ari had read about the use of airplanes in that war, although it had nothing to do with Mr. Hallstadt. It sounded like Ari was about to get to the actual story when I felt a tug on my sleeve. It was Mr. Sadler pulling me back towards a corner of the room.

"What's up?" I asked, thinking perhaps he wanted to change something about the story he had told me.

In response, I felt an envelope being pushed into my hand. I didn't even have to look down to know what it was.

Mr. Sadler looked at me. "I didn't take Mr. Hargreaves' fifty dollars, and I don't have to take your $10,000."

"But why?" I asked. I did not like being compared to Mr. Hargreaves. "It's for the Center. To fix it up."

He looked at me hard. "I can't tell you where I got it," I said. "I just can't. But it's mine. Really. I got it honestly."

"Why'd you bring it?" I could feel Mr. Sadler's eyes inspecting me like a chef turning a potato around to make sure that there were no blemishes.

"To leave it here where someone I could trust would find it. Why won't you take it? I really want the center to have it. Your story meant a lot to me."

Mr. Sadler took the envelope back from my hand and tucked it into his trouser pocket. "Yes, I will take it. Do you want to know why?" I nodded. I was so confused. "You came with a big packet of money," he said. "You were going to help us even before you met us. Even before you knew who we were. Well, that's just not right. It makes the money into nothing but money. If you want it to be more than that, then you'd better get to know us first."

"How could money be anything except money?" I asked, puzzled.

"It can be love. Respect. Guilt. Contempt. Even hatred. But money is never just money."

He shook my hand and pushed me forward gently with his thin, thin hand. Ms. Floyd was finishing with Amanda who apparently had just given her presentation. As I approached, I was surprised to hear what Ms. Floyd was saying: "That is just not acceptable, Amanda. I didn't say anything when you took advantage of your friends this morning, or when you snuck out instead of helping here. But that is just plain rude to our hosts, and I will not stand for it. Now go back to Mrs. Cromley, apologize, and actually talk with her. And Lydia, if the story you have to tell exhibits the same sort of disrespect, then you'd better go back right now to Mr. Alma and do a better job." Turning to the audience, Ms. Floyd pulled herself together. "I do apologize. Those are not students typical of Oakes Middle School."

"Don't apologize, dear," said Ms. Markson. "We quite enjoyed it. In fact, you were too gentle on her."

"Now," said Ms. Floyd, consulting her list, "Jake Richter will tell you a story from the life of Thomas Sadler."

I stood. "They called him 'Beech,'" I began, "and he is the grandchild of slaves."

I saw Mr. Sadler touch the handkerchief in his pocket.

Chapter 14

Whenever we went into the city by ourselves, my parents gave me the same lecture: Call if we need help, don't go anywhere with strangers, be careful of the crazy drivers. This time, just as I was leaving, my father put a ten dollar bill in my hand. "Put that in a safe place, just in case of emergencies." I thanked him, shoved it into my pocket, and left.

It's not like the city is that big a place to begin with. But compared to the other towns in the area, it definitely deserved the title "city." It had its own trolley system, homeless people on the street, and a section called "The Red Zone" where kids our age get really uncomfortable with what's on the movie marquees.

I had agreed to pick up Mimi on my way to the train station even though it was in the wrong direction because I had a special mission. As I stood outside my house, I checked the contents of the envelope again. It was a plain brown envelope. I'd wrapped the bills inside with some of the special pink yarn my mother was using to knit a cap for Maddie. It had flecks of green and purple in it, and little sparkly bits, too, but it's what was handy. I licked the flap and made sure it was sealed, and carefully zipped the envelope inside my coat. I didn't want $20,000 in thousand dollar bills falling out into the street as I biked.

I approached Mimi's house carefully, and snuck up to her mailbox, checking to see if anyone was looking. I put the envelope in and closed the lid trying not to make a sound.

Then I knocked on Mimi's door, probably louder than usual.

Mimi came out dressed in a green t-shirt, darker green shorts, green sneakers, and pink socks. You couldn't get much spring-ier than that. "Hi," she said as she stepped past me on the stoop in front of her door. Then, as if remembering something she'd forgotten, she turned back and flipped up the lid of the mailbox. She took out the envelope, looked at it, said, "Odd. No stamp," opened her front door, and put it on the mail table. We headed off to the station. I was relieved. I didn't want to tell Mimi about the gift until after her parents got it just in case she didn't like the idea. But I also didn't want her to hear about it from her parents instead of from me. Some time today I figured I'd have a chance to tell her without Ari being around.

Now was not to be that time. Ari came scooting up on his bike, lightly crashed into Mimi's porch rail, and turned around so that together we could ride the six blocks to the train station.

• • •

We talked for the entire 35 minute trip, except for ten minutes when we went to the refreshment car where we ate terrible muffins. Mainly we talked about how we were going to spend money in the city. That was our mission. Away from our parents and other friends, we could at last just be plain old rich kids.

The city is the last stop the train makes, which is one reason our parents let us take it: it's hard to get off at the wrong place. We emerged into the fresh air like people waking up. The day had a little bite of cold to it, making the city seem even more filled with straight lines and corners than usual.

"Where to first?" I asked, patting my front pockets, each of which held a ridiculous amount of money. I'd split the cash up, figuring I wouldn't get pickpocketed in both pockets.

"The Planetarium!" said Ari without hesitation. Mimi and I looked at each other. Why not?

"It's this way," said Mimi, heading up the street. She was by far the best oriented of the three of us.

"Walking?" I said in mock shock. "Never!" I stepped to the curb and waved my hand. A taxi pulled up.

Now, there are some things about being a kid with money that you're not ready for. I was expecting the cab driver to look at us as if we were spoiled brats. And since we were in the city in order to act like spoiled brats, we deserved that look. After all, the driver was working hard all day in order to make the sort of money that we were just throwing around. But what I wasn't ready for was tipping. I knew that you usually tip 15% of the cost of the ride. And I could do the math. The problem is that it's just plain embarrassing to give someone a tip. It's not so bad when you can leave it on a table and flee, but when you have to actually hand it to someone, they get to see if you're a big tipper or a little tipper.

So, I sat during the entire drive worrying about the moment of truth. As we got close to the planetarium, it was clear that the ride was going to cost about $6.00. Fifteen percent is ten percent plus half of ten percent. That's 90 cents. Round it up to a dollar. Total cost of ride, including tip: $7.00. Easy. But the smallest bill I had was a ten. So, I'd give him the ten and ask for three back. But what's $3 to the world's richest boy? I should just say, "Keep the change," except then I would really seem like a spoiled rich kid. But the driver wouldn't care: I may be spoiled, but I tip well. Those three dollars might mean something to the driver. On the other hand, I could give him a twenty dollar bill and tell him to keep the change and it wouldn't make the slightest bit of difference to me. But he'd look at the twenty and ask me if I meant to give him a ten. "No, no, keep the change, my good man," I'd say. No, giving him a twenty would draw out the entire interchange. I could give him the twenty and then run away, but suppose he started chasing me, waving the $20 bill and yelling "Hey, Spoiled Rich Kid, you gave me too much money!" So much to think about.

So, I sat there, chewing my lip, dreading the moment when I'd have to pay. My anxiety was clearly bothering Mimi and Ari also.

The cab pulled to the curb. "Six dollars even," said the taxi driver.

"You did a very nice job," I said, handing him a twenty dollar bill. "Keep the change."

He looked at it carefully, nodded once and drove off without saying a word and without looking back.

• • •

The planetarium was fun. It always is. Even if you don't care about the universe – although, if you don't care about the universe, what's left to care about? – it's just such a cool place. It's darker than dark, and then the stars come out, and a big voice comes over the loudspeakers from all directions at once. Plus, they always have some show biz touch. This time it was a race through the solar system faster than the speed of light, taking a left around Jupiter and a couple of spins around Neptune.

We went to the museum's gift store but didn't want to get anything too expensive that we couldn't explain to our parents, so I got a selection of little things: some polished gems, a light-up pen, and a foam "moon rock."

Next it was on to the Mystery Arcade, the largest electronic game place in the city. The three of us had put in plenty of hours at the Quarter Time arcade in our town. Quarter Time was a single room in the mall with machines lining its walls. At the Mystery Arcade, you left the electronic fighting machine room and you entered the electronic fake sports room, which was to the right of the electronic pinball room. And that was just on the first floor. The three of us stood in awe, frozen in the entry way. Then I headed for the change machine.

Do you know how much $50 in quarters weighs? More than you think. But after I divided it into threes (Ari and Mimi each got an extra), they didn't feel heavy, just comforting. We played and played, sometimes together, sometimes apart, until our brains were booping with electronic beeps and our fingers were flicking without our even wanting them to.

Even after we'd sat on the bench outside for ten minutes, we could still feel the ringing in our brains. "Where to?" I asked.

Mimi looked hesitant. "What is it?" I asked.

"I sort of read about an exhibit at the Museum of Art

that sounded sort of cool. Would you be sort of interested in going?"

"Sort of," I replied. "What is it?"

"Well, it's this woman who takes pictures of everyday things really close up so you can see their textures."

"Whatever!" Ari said enthusiastically.

"Taxi!" I called.

• • •

Why do museums have such large doors? What sort of giants do they think are going to be visiting?

Before stepping through them, we wanted to have a snack. Rather than waiting in a restaurant, we decided to eat from the food carts in front of the museum: roasted chestnuts, hot sugared cashews, a Super Sluggo ice cream bar and sodas all around. It was more than we could eat. In fact, it was more than we could hold. We sat on a bench, leaning forward to avoid the dripping ice cream, and ate until we were full. Then we closed up the bags of cashews and carefully placed the rest of our uneaten treats into a waste basket where a squirrel was happily feasting regardless of the large mammals next to him.

The line into the museum was short, and we had barely wiped our hands on the napkins when it was our turn. Immediately I was facing another crisis, for the sign at the booth said

ADMISSION
———————————————————
DONATE WHATEVER YOU WANT

Suggestion:
$7.00 for adults and
$2.00 for children under 12

"Wow, it's free!" said Ari.

"That's so unfair," said Mimi at the same time.

"Why unfair?"

"Because you have to decide whether you're going to be a cheapskate."

"That's why they have the suggestion," I said.

"But it's just a suggestion."

"That's what they expect you to pay."

"No it's not. That's why they call it a suggestion."

I turned to the woman in the booth. "Excuse me, but do most people pay the $7?"

She had been listening to our discussion and smiled. "About half do."

"And does the other half go in for free?" asked Ari, a little too eagerly?

"Some do. Some people put in more. Some put in a few dollars, depending on what they can afford."

"Thank you," I said and stepped out of the line so that other people, less confused than we were, could enter. The three of us stood next to a giant statue of a man, a woman and a child made entirely out of nails.

"So, let's pay our money and go in," Mimi said.

"You heard her," I said. "Some people pay less depending on what they can afford, and some people pay more."

"So?" asked Ari.

"Do you know what I could afford?"

"So pay $10 each and let's go in," said Ari.

"Why $10?"

"Because it's more and it's not $11.37."

"What's wrong with $11.37?" I asked.

"It's not round. No one gives un-round numbers, unless they're putting in all their change."

"So why not $20?"

"Ok, $20," Ari said. "Let's go in."

I shook my head. "I don't know how to figure this out."

Mimi put her hand on my shoulder and said, "There's nothing to figure. There are no rules. You're the world's richest boy. You're an exception to the rules about money."

"So, what do I do?"

"Put in a thousand dollars."

"What?!" Ari said, in shock. "A thousand dollars? Why?!"

"Because he can without even noticing it. You brought that much, didn't you?"

"Plenty more than that," I said, feeling both front pockets to reassure myself that the money was still there.

"So, a thousand dollars is nice round number."

"So why not two thousand?"

"Because, well, that's too much," Mimi said with such decisiveness that ended the conversation.

I turned away so I could pull out a thousand dollar bill without attracting attention, folded the bill up so you couldn't see how much it was for, and strolled casually back to the booth. As if I were just dropping in a couple of bucks, I dropped it into the slot and walked in. Mimi and Ari each put in a $10 bill I'd given them.

No one noticed. When they counted the money up that evening, I imagined someone saying, "Hey, Myrtle, that's one generous person!"

Of course, I'd never know. And I'd never be thanked. That shouldn't have mattered to me, but, strangely, it did. A little.

• • •

We stepped out into the light with a half day left. The museum had been a museum: walls and walls of stuff I didn't care about with occasional items that carried me like a crumb being washed down a drain. The rooms with the photo exhibit were good. Because the photographer had taken pictures of things in extreme close-up, you had to stand back from the wall to see what they were, but as you got closer and closer, the textures of the thing became more interesting. So, like everyone else there, we walked backwards and forwards in front of each photo as if we were on a rubber band.

When we got outside, we realized we were hungry again. That junk food feast hadn't filled us up for long. I opened up the tourist information I'd gotten from the Web. "Grande Fleur," I said, pointing at the entry. "That's where we're going to have lunch. Taxi!"

The tourist guide said that the Grande Fleur was the finest

restaurant in town, featuring French menu items that I couldn't have pronounced even if I'd had my jaw hinges oiled. The service was reported to be perfect, with waiters in white gloves attending to your every need. The décor – the insides – was described as opulent and elegant, which I figured meant that they didn't have photos of the owner's nieces and nephews on the wall. But it didn't matter because the Grande Fleur was full. No amount of money was going to empty the place any sooner.

"You want to wait or find somewhere else?" I asked.

"I'm getting hungry," said Ari.

So, we looked in the guide again. The Salzburg Grille was ranked almost as high as the Grande Fleur and it was only a couple of blocks away. It was a beautiful day and spending money on a cab to go two blocks didn't even feel like fun, so we walked.

"There it is," I said. The Salzburg Grille has a dark blue awning with its name written in gold script. Two doors before it was a jewelry store that had gone out of business. The lights were off and the store was empty. Sitting on a blanket in its doorway were a homeless woman and a man and a little dog. A sign written on a crinkled flap from a cardboard box said "Homeless and hungry. Give a hand?" Probably because we were kids, they didn't look at us as we approached. "Oh, look at the dog," said Mimi, giving me a wide-eyed tender gaze.

"I don't know," I said, panicked, in a soft voice. I didn't want to be forced into a decision right away. "Stay away," I said, "and we'll talk about it at lunch."

"But…"

"Please," I said urgently. "I don't want to talk about it in front of them."

We waved and passed by. "Cute dog," Mimi said to them. They smiled back at her.

The restaurant was beautiful, all brick and brass and plants. The waiter who seated us only looked at us funny for a moment, and then must have figured that our parents had sent us here with money. His hair was slicked back, he wore a white shirt that was so clean and white it would probably have stayed lit even if the lights went out, and he walked so straight you could tear paper along his edge. "Right this way," he said, leading us to a table near the window looking out on the homeless couple.

"I don't feel good about this," said Mimi. "Those people are hungry and here we are…" We looked at the menus silently. Even the appetizers cost more than ten dollars. I did the math and figured we'd be spending about $150 here. Although that wasn't even a drop in my bucket, it was still a lot of money to spend on a lunch for three.

"Ok, Mimi, I don't feel good about it either. But whatever we do, it doesn't have to affect our lunch. It's not like I have $150 that I can spend either on lunch or on them. So, let's order a nice lunch. I'm really hungry."

"Me, too," said Ari, putting half a roll into his mouth all at once, and, worse, leaving the other half sticking out from his mouth.

The waiter who had seated us came over and said that it

was going to be his pleasure to serve us this afternoon. (Yeah, I thought, if it's such a pleasure, why do they have to pay him to do it?) It turns out that the Salzburg Grille is a grill, and grills feature meat, making it tough to order an all-vegetarian meal. But we managed: French fries, salads, grilled cheese, fried mozzarella sticks, onion rings, a portabella mushroom sandwich, ginger broccoli stir fry, garlic bread, stuffed potatoes and brownie sundaes for dessert.

As we waited for the food to arrive, Mimi tapped out a rhythm with a breadstick. "So what are we going to do for those nice people?" she asked.

"How do you know they're nice?" asked Ari.

"Because they smiled when I complimented their doggie. Besides, the doggie looks happy and friendly, so they must take good care of it, which can't be easy when you're homeless and begging on the streets."

"He didn't look that happy to me," Ari protested.

"I can tell," said Mimi.

"You *think* you can tell."

"It doesn't matter if the dog is nice," I interrupted.

"You're going to give them money anyway?" asked Ari.

"Yes. Maybe. I don't know yet." I was thinking about what "Beech" Sadler had told me: I should know who they are instead of just dropping money in their lap.

When the waiter brought our food, I ordered three hamburgers to go, except they of course don't call them "hamburgers" in a place like the Salzburg Grille. No, they were "ground porterhouse," and you had to ask to get ketchup.

"We don't generally prepare take-out meals," the waiter said. "I'm so sorry."

No he wasn't.

As he was about to turn away, I said, "Ok. Do you do doggy bags if we can't finish our lunch?"

"Yes, certainly, sir, we can packaged your uneaten portion for home consumption." He didn't look happy that I had called them doggy bags.

"In that case, I'd like three hamburgers to eat now because I'm really really hungry. And if I can't finish them, I'll ask you to pack them up for me in a doggy bag."

"Why don't I just put them in a carry-away carton for you and have it ready for you when you're done with your meal?"

"Good idea! Thank you."

And when we were done, there was our waiter with the bill. Only after I had paid in full did he hand over the bag with the three hamburger lunches in it. "Thank you," I said, leaving a $100 tip. No, I didn't like him very much, but he was working hard.

• • •

I still wasn't sure how much I was going to give the homeless couple when Mimi began petting their dog. The dog got all excited the way little dogs do, skittering about on his little dog feet as if the sidewalk were just too hot to stand still on. "What's his name?" she asked.

"Spunky," said the man.

"Short for Spunkalator," explained the woman.

"He's adorable," Mimi said.

"He's a good dog," confirmed the man.

Mimi looked at me and said to the couple, "We were wondering if you and Spunky would like some hamburgers from that restaurant." I stepped forward with the bag.

"From the Grille? Sure! I've always wondered what their food is like."

I handed the bag to him and he carefully laid out its contents: fat hamburgers on hard rolls, a container of ketchup, a large bag of French fries (or, as the Grille called them, "Crisp Juliennes of New Potatoes"), thick paper napkins and three heavy-weight plastic forks as if anyone would use forks to eat French fries and hamburgers. He pulled at one meat patty until a large chunk came off and gave it to Spunky. It was gone in two shakes of a small dog's tail.

"Oh, he likes that," said the woman.

"This is a very nice thing you've done," said the man. "This is our regular spot, but I've never had food from there."

"It's good," said Ari.

The man took a bite. "Hmm, yes it is. It's very good."

"Do you want some?" the woman asked.

"Oh no," Mimi said. "We just ate. Thanks though." Also, she was a vegetarian.

"So," said Ari as the three of them ate their hamburgers,

"How'd you end up here?"

It's good to have Ari with you if you want something blurted out.

"Not that you're 'ending up' here," said Mimi, awkwardly.

"No, no," said the man. "That's a fair question. And the answer is pretty simple."

"I'm schizophrenic," said the woman. "My name is Caroline."

"I'm Philip," said the man, and we introduced ourselves to him.

"Yes," said Philip, "Caroline is schizophrenic. Do you know what that means?"

"She thinks she's different people," Ari said with all the confidence that ignorance can give a person.

"No, that's what it means in the movies. But in real life, a schizophrenic is, well, a crazy person. Caroline sometimes hears voices that aren't there."

"Not in a while."

"Not in a couple of days," Philip said. "And when she hears voices, she talks back to them."

"Yeah, I'm nuts," Caroline said. "It scares me."

"Can't they do anything about it?"

"Not much," said Caroline. "You know the Carlton Center? I was there for a couple of years. And then the state stopped paying so they kicked me out."

"They just put you on the street?"

"They tried to help. I was supposed to come in every week or every two weeks or something, but I kept getting confused. Never made it back. But then I met Philip and Spunky."

"I was living on the street," Philip said. "And it's easy to tell you how I got there: drugs. I was a heroin addict. I probably still am."

"Don't you know?" asked Ari.

"I'm not using now, but I may be tomorrow. That's the sad truth. Can't get a job and couldn't keep one if I did. I've tried and I always end up back using. It's a bad thing, but I guess they teach you that in school."

"Yeah, we did a whole unit on it in Health," Ari said a tad too cheerfully. I looked harshly at him to keep him from describing the report he'd done. It had been in the form of a humorous skit.

"So now you both live on the street and live on what people give you?" I asked.

"Sometimes we save enough money to get ourselves a little treat," said Caroline.

"Mainly we just drink up the extra money, to tell you the truth."

"That's not true, Philly. We got this sweater for me with money we saved."

"That was over a year ago," Philip said gently.

"So," I asked, "What would you do if you won the

lottery?"

"How much?"

"Say $10,000."

"Well, that'd be too much to drink," said Philip.

"I'd stay in a hotel and get room service," said Caroline.

"I'd invite our friends. Have a party."

"Fun!" said Caroline.

"Or, we could try to get off the streets," Philip said, rubbing his chin. He pulled Spunky into his lap and stroked his head and back. "That'd be the smart thing to do. Of course, I didn't get here by doing smart things."

"Oh, don't say that," said Caroline.

"Hard to say anything else," Philip replied. "So, what would get me off the street? I could get myself cleaned up with that type of money. Some new clothes so I wouldn't look like a bum. We could rent a little place. Maybe I could get a job if I didn't look homeless."

"A lot of it is the clothing," Caroline confided.

"I could get a cell phone so I could apply for a job and give them a way to reach me. But I haven't been good at holding jobs," he continued.

I looked at Mimi. She nodded. "Ok, this is going to be hard to believe," I began, "but I want you to have this." I pulled an envelope out of each of my front pockets. "That's $10,000." I held it out to them. They didn't move. "It's for you. You can't tell anyone where you got it, but it's totally legal."

"He won the lottery. The big one," said Ari. "Really."

"Really I did. I won more money than anyone could spend in a lifetime. So, please take this. But I hope you don't spend it on a hotel room or…" I didn't want to say "heroin."

Caroline took one envelope from my hand. Philip looked at her and then took the other envelope. They looked in them as if they were peering through a telescope at another world.

"I don't know what to say," said Philip.

"It's really awkward for all of us," I said.

"Not for me," said Caroline. "Thank you. Thank you."

"Thank you," said Philip. "We'll try to do something with this."

"Spunky thanks you," said Caroline, waving the dog's tiny paw at us.

"Ok. You're welcome. And remember, you can't tell anyone where you got it."

"Won't tell a soul."

We were backing away when someone approached the blanket they were sitting on and dropped a bill into the couple's cup. "Thanks, Martin," said Caroline. "Ooh," she said. "It's a twenty! He must have had a good day."

"He's a regular. Everyday he drops in a buck or two," explained Philip.

As Martin continued down the street, we saw that he had been our waiter at lunch.

. . .

"Well, I feel really weird about that," I said when we were a block away.

"About what?" Ari asked.

"About giving them the money."

"I know what you mean," said Mimi. "It's just so weird that you have so much and they have nothing. And you get to decide."

"Yeah. I could have given them $5,000 or $15,000. No difference to me. A huge difference to them."

"Or you could have given them $12,000," chimed in Ari

"Uh huh."

"Or $16,300," he said.

"Ok, Ari, we got the point."

I wanted Ari to stop before he said, "Or $20,000." That's what I gave Mimi's family. My stomach knotted as I thought about how Mimi would react when she found out that I'd given her parents money as if they were a couple living on the street.

We walked down the street, not in the mood for a taxi, until we got to the Barrymore Theatre in the center of the city. I chatted about everything I could think of in order to keep the topic off of charity and money. When we got to the theatre, I ordered three of the best seats for the matinee performance of "Magic and All That," a show that combined magic and comedy. With Ari between me and Mimi, I felt safer, but even so I read the program guide studiously until the lights went down to avoid talking with her. I just felt awkward. And I hoped the feeling would go away soon.

At intermission, Ari went to get candy. The seat was getting uncomfortable, so I stood. "Mimi," I said, "there's something I have to tell you."

She looked up, waiting.

"You know that envelope in your mailbox this morning? The one without any stamps?" She nodded. "That was from me. I gave your parents some money to help them out. But you can't tell them it was from me."

"How much?" she asked. Her voice was neutral, like she was asking how much a candy bar cost.

"I didn't know how much would be right, so I gave them $20,000."

She didn't say anything,

"So," I asked, "what do you think?"

"What do you want me to think?"

"Nothing," I replied, confused.

"Ok, I think nothing. You did it. It's done. I won't give away your secret."

Ari came back with six candy bars. "I didn't know what you'd want, so I got one of each."

The show was good but not great: many of the tricks were familiar – he actually sawed a lady in half – and the comedy sketches were sort of dumb. Nevertheless, as we left I found myself saying "That was great! Fantastic!" because I had discovered, in the program guide, the right way to give away money.

Mimi didn't speak to either of us during the entire ride home.

"She must be tired," Ari said to me.

I didn't reply.

Chapter 15

The Fordgythe Foundation
HELPING WITH A HELPING HAND
PO Box 1274 • MELVILLE

That's what it said on the stationery I had ordered over the Internet. I picked up the carton at my new post office box and didn't open it until I was back in my bedroom. The cream colored pages were heavy, and you could read the raised lettering with your fingers if you had to. It even smelled good, like fresh laundry. I hid the paper by putting it in the middle of the stack of reams of paper for my computer.

What a world: Print up some stationery and you have your own business. If I were really creating the Fordgythe Foundation, I'd probably have to do some stuff with a lawyer. But I was just going to give away money, and there's no law against that. At least none that anyone ever told me about.

From downstairs came a "Grrrr." If I hadn't recognized my father's voice, I might have thought a bear had moved in. Or possibly a large electric razor.

"What's Dad grrrr-ing about?" I asked my mother. She was correcting papers her class had handed in. You usually don't think about the teacher at home, sitting at a table grading while the rest of her life goes on around her.

"*The Register* has come out in favor of the state spending even more money advertising the lottery," Mom said.

"Grrrr," my father explained.

Even though my one experience with the state lottery was pretty good, to put it mildly, I still would have voted against the state having one. But it never was to me a tenth the big deal that it was to my father. It sure got my father mad. Worse, I had a good hunch that Mr. Dunn had made *The Register* endorse more lottery advertising just to make my father angry. And it had worked.

I went back upstairs and took some recent copies of *The Gazette* with me. I was looking for people who could use the helping hand of the Fordgythe Institute. After all, we are the Helping Hand People. About an hour later, I biked down to the bank and had a nice chat with Ms. Harrigan, the woman who opened the account for me when I first won the lottery. I'd grown to trust her. For example, here's the conversation we had that afternoon.

Me: Hello, Ms. Harrigan.

Ms. Harrigan: Good afternoon, Jake! Such a pleasure to see you. Such a pleasure.

Met: Thank you. It's nice seeing you, too.

Ms. Harrigan: What can I help you with this afternoon?

Me: Well, I had an idea.

Ms. Harrigan: Good. I like ideas. I *like* ideas.

Me: I had this stationery printed up.

Ms. Harrigan: Very nice! Very, very nice! Did you design this yourself?

Me: Yeah. Well, I sort of stole it from the Web. I found a template.

162

Ms. Harrigan: Was it for sale?

Me; Not really. They said you could use it for free.

Ms. Harrigan: Not really stealing then, is it? Not stealing at all. So, you're starting a foundation. What an excellent idea! Excellent!

Me: Am I allowed to?

Ms. Harrigan: I don't see why not. Are you going to cheat anyone? Defraud them? Trick them out of their money and their houses?

Me: No! I'm going to give them money that they really need.

Ms. Harrigan: Excellent. Excellent! That sounds like so much fun! Fun! And how much do you need this afternoon?

Me: I was thinking I'd start with $50,000.

Ms. Harrigan: In hundreds? Thousands?

Me: I think thousands would be best.

Ms. Harrigan: Excellent. Excellent. Could you just wait here for a minute and I'll go get the forms and the cash? Just for a minute.

Me: Thank you.

Ms. Harrigan: No, thank *you*. And there's a copy of *People* magazine there if you'd like to read it. *People*.

Three minutes later, she came back with an envelope with fifty $1,000 bills in it. I didn't even count it because if you can't trust Ms. Harrigan, then who can you trust? Who can you trust?

You can be sure that when I tucked that envelope into my backpack, I made double-sure the backpack was completely zipped up and that the straps weren't going to break. I really didn't want to have to explain why I was chasing thousand dollar bills blowing down the street.

When I got home, I closed my door and moved the money into the Fordgythe envelopes I'd had printed up, being sure that only a little of the money was exposed at any one time, just in case someone barged into my room. Once the money was sorted, I just as carefully tied each envelope with the pink and purple and green and sparkly yarn I'd snagged from my mother. I wanted the money to look festive, after all. Then I printed names out on my computer on sticky-backed labels and made sure I had the right names on the right envelopes. When I was done, I put the white envelopes back into the big envelope from the bank, and zipped it all up into my backpack.

I was ready.

My first stop was obvious. I bicycled past the front of Dunn Village three times, making sure that none of the people I had met there was in the front driveway or looking out the windows. I especially didn't want to run into Mr. Beecher. I could picture him lassoing me off of my bike. But there were no signs of activity, so on my fourth pass, I stopped in front of their mailbox and shoved the envelope into it. Inside was a carefully typed letter telling them that the Fordgythe Foundation had awarded them $30,000 to be used for the betterment of the building and to provide services to those who use the building...I'd read up on how foundations talk. And I rode away quickly but calmly, I hoped. My heart was beating fast, but not from biking.

I was on my way to Ms. Floyd's house when Ari flagged me down. I pulled up next to him on the street. "What's up?" I asked. I could tell he was upset because he alternated between pulling up his pants and pushing back his glasses.

"Amanda and Roger broke up!"

Oh no, I thought. "Hey, that's great," I said.

"Lydia told me. She said I should make my move."

I could imagine Lydia's sarcastic tone of voice.

"She really meant it," Ari said, as if reading my mind. I was impressed. He usually wasn't that aware of what people were thinking. "She said she'd help me."

"Why would she help you?"

"Because she's angry at Amanda."

"Really?" I asked. I think my left eyebrow probably went up. It does that sometimes.

"Yeah. Roger broke up with Amanda so he could start going with Balia." Balia was a pretty girl in class who wasn't a complete jerk. Now I had a little less respect for her.

"So why does she want you to move in on Amanda? That doesn't make sense."

"Yes it does. It's because....Ok, so no it doesn't. But who cares? She wants to help me. She's going to meet me in half an hour. Can you come?"

"Yeah, sure. I just have to drop this off at Ms. Floyd's."

"Ms. Floyd's getting a Fordgythe grant?"

"Yeah. I think she's a good teacher."

"Me, too."

"So, grant city here she comes!"

"How much?"

I don't know why I got embarrassed. "Some. Doesn't matter."

Ari rode with me over to Ms. Floyd's apartment. The building was nothing special, but I liked that it was an apartment because it meant that anybody watching couldn't tell exactly which mailbox I put the envelope into. As we left, I turned to see the tip of the white envelope visible through the slot. I hoped it made her a little happy.

Lydia was waiting for us in a booth at the Soda Squirt. The table was piled with books and notebooks, as if Lydia were studying simultaneously for nine exams. This was not the "Who cares? Whatever!" Lydia I had grown to know and dislike.

"Hey, Lydia," I said, but before the words were out of my mouth, she was telling us to take all the books from our backpacks.

"Look like you're tutoring me or something," she whispered urgently. And then I understood why she had all her study materials on display: she didn't want anyone to think she was actually having a social meeting with low-lifes like Ari and me. We were just too unpopular to be seen with.

We took out some books. As I pretended to be looking something up in my geology textbook and Ari was doing some cross-referencing in his Spanish book, I said, "So, why do you want to help Ari with Amanda?"

"It's just so annoying!" she said. She sighed once, heavily. "Amanda obviously has to have another boyfriend, immediamento."

"Obviously."

"She can't be seen as a loser. Ari here is out of the question, of course."

Ari looked up from his Spanish book. He'd been looking up "immediamento." I could have told him that it wasn't in there.

"At least as a long-term boyfriend," Lydia added. "But there's a gala at the Dunn Fairways golf course this weekend and Amanda has to go. And Mr. Dunn liked something about Ari when he met him at his house. He said to her, 'How about that short boy with the funny hair? He seemed to like you.' She said no, but finally Mr. Dunn got his way. So, it looks like Ari gets his shot."

"Really?" he said, pleased. Clearly all the bad things Lydia had said along the way hadn't registered. To him, it was like the end of a four-day drive to Disneyworld, when the sight of the Magic Castle erases the tortures of sitting in the back, strapped in next to your annoying sister Maddie.

"Yeah," Lydia said. Then, turning to me, she added, "Can you clean him up?"

"I showered yesterday!" Ari protested.

"Can you help us?" I asked. "I'm not really sure what Amanda looks for in a cleaned-up boy."

"Yeah. I guess," Lydia said, putting a couple of packets of fake sugar into her pocketbook. We agreed to go into the city together after school on Wednesday.

Lydia stayed in the Soda Squirt while Ari and I left so she wouldn't be caught exiting a public place with the likes of us. Charming.

We were just turning the corner when we saw Mimi looking in the window of Charms 'n Gold, a jewelry store.

"Hi, Mimi."

"Mmm."

"Are you ok?"

"Fine," she said, continuing to stare in the window. I doubted that the charm bracelets and ankle bracelets really interested her that much.

Rather than asking her again whether she was ok, I said, "Jewelry shopping? I didn't think you wear jewelry."

She turned to look at me. "My father got his job back."

"That's great!"

"Hey," said Ari, positively.

"Yeah, it's great," Mimi said without enthusiasm.

"What's wrong, Mimi? You don't sound happy about it."

"I'm happy he got his job back. But …"

"But what?"

"It was nice of you to try to help him out, I guess. But it really messed him up."

"It did? How?"

"It was so out of the blue. He was confused. Where did it come from? Why him? Was it a trick by Mr. Dunn? Was it legal? Was someone trying to trap him? And when he didn't think it was a trick, his pride was hurt. He's never taken charity before."

"I didn't …"

"I know. But he was already upset about being fired. He wouldn't spend a penny of it."

"Oh no."

"And then he got his job back, so he put the money into the bank. And he gave me $50 to buy myself something here. And, no, I don't like jewelry, but it looks like I'll have to get something."

When Mimi started to cry, I figured it wasn't because she was being forced to buy jewelry. It must have been so hard to live in her house over the past week, and my gift had made it harder. I felt terrible. "I only wanted to help," I said.

"I know. It's not your fault. I shouldn't have been angry. But you could have asked me first."

"I was afraid you'd say no."

A few minutes later, Mimi, Ari and I walked out of the store with a gold necklace with a gold dolphin hanging from it that Mimi liked even though she went into the store determined not to like anything. I had to pay an extra $29 for it because $50 turned out not to be enough.

"I'll pay you back," said Mimi.

"Oh, Mimi, please don't." I knew she was saying that because she was still angry at me. I started to figure out how long it takes me to earn $29 in interest, but stopped since that wasn't the point at all.

• • •

"My father's paper is in trouble," I said as we walked home. "Advertising is down. Mr. Dunn has been lowering the price of advertising in *The Register*."

"Well, we could make up more ads," Mimi suggested. "That'd help replace the advertisers who go with *The Register* instead."

When we got to my house, Ari asked, "Can I do the first one? I have a really good idea. It'll just take me three minutes."

Half an hour later, Mimi and I paused our video game and checked back in. (I was happy to have an excuse to stop because Mimi was kicking my butt. I have the reflexes of a tired amoeba.) "Almost done," Ari said. "Another three minutes."

When we came up next time, he was printing out what he'd written. In bold black print it said: "Go Grangers! We Love Ya!" The Grangers are our high school's baseball team. Underneath there was a drawing of a bowling ball knocking down some pins. "That's the only picture I could find," Ari said.

"Well, that's a start," Mimi said.

"Aren't people going to wonder who placed the ad?" I asked.

"They'll just figure it was some school group."

We quickly printed out another three ads supporting local

teams, local charities, and the Selma Todd Day celebrations when everyone in town is supposed to plant a flower. None said anything about who was donating the money for the ads.

"You know, there are only so many public service announcements we can run," I said. "We need to come up with something that sounds like a business but that no one can check on."

We sat for about thirty seconds before Ari said, "We could pretend to be opening a bank."

"But what happens when someone goes to the pretend bank and finds there's nothing there?"

"Oh."

Another 30 seconds.

"We could run an ad for a real bank."

"I think they'd be touchy about that. They'd come to my father, wanting to know who placed the ad."

We waited 45 seconds.

Ari snapped his fingers. "We could make up companies. Like the Ace Flower Shop and Nose Repair."

"And what happens when someone reads the ad and wants to buy something from there?" I said.

At just about the same time, Mimi said, "What the heck is nose repair?"

"If you break your nose," Ari said defensively.

"Their motto could be, 'The place to come if you don't smell so good,'" Mimi said.

"The one good thing about that idea," I said, "is that no one would go to the store."

"Why would that be good?" Ari asked.

"Because there's no such store," Mimi reminded him.

"Ex-Post, the store for used fence posts," I said. "Nobody wants used fence posts."

Two cars outside seemed to be engaged in a honking contest. We sat. I rooted for the one that made a Braaaaaat sound like a whoopee cushion.

"Horning In," I said, "We'll replace your car's honk with whatever you record."

"So your car horn will be you yelling some rude remark? That sounds like a good idea," said Mimi.

"Then we can't use it."

"How about Third Grade Masterpieces: copies of famous paintings by third graders. And we could write in small print that it was the stuff that their own parents didn't want," Mimi suggested.

"Refrigerator Organizers: We'll come to your house and organize the stuff stuck on your refrigerator with magnets," Ari said.

"How about Acme Photo Fresh Cement?" suggested Mimi. "The place to take your pictures of fresh cement. We specialize so you're guaranteed the best fresh cement photos anywhere."

Ari interrupted the a few seconds of silence excitedly: "Cow

Chip Cookies!"

"Aren't cow chips what cows leave in the field" Mimi asked.

"Yeah! That's why no one will want them!"

"I bet we'd get some orders from practical jokers. People are just crazy," Mimi said. "It's got to be something that absolutely no one would want."

"Freddy's Cow Chip String," said Ari.

"That doesn't even mean anything," Mimi said. She was drawing circles on her blue jeans. They'd probably come out in the wash.

"They're string for stringing together cow chips, and they come from Freddy," Ari said defensively.

"This isn't working," I finally said.

"Nope," said Mimi, agreeing. (That's one of the few times when "Nope" means you agree.)

"We just need to think harder," said Ari.

"No we don't. We need to give up," I said.

"Acme Bird Wrappers?" Ari asked.

Mimi and I looked at each other, sighed, and gave up.

Chapter 16

It was Wednesday and this time there were four of us going in to the city: Ari, Mimi, me and Lydia. Our mission: to get Ari outfitted well enough to look like a boy Amanda might actually go to a social event with. It was a challenge that even $100,000,000 might not be enough to meet.

I had given Mimi $50 before we left and Ari $500 so that Lydia wouldn't catch on that I was the Sugar Plum Fairy when it comes to money. "That's too much!" said Ari when I'd handed him the cash.

"I hope so," I said. "But you should spend as much of it as you need."

"Won't Lydia get suspicious?"

"No," Mimi said, pocketing her $50. "She's so spoiled she probably doesn't have any idea how much things cost or what a reasonable amount to spend is. She just assumes everyone has enough money to afford anything."

"That's why she stuck me with the bill at the Soda Squirt the other day," I said. "I thought she was being cheap, but she was really just being spoiled."

"Oh, that's a lot better," said Mimi.

"Don't ever lose that girlish sarcasm," I said to her sarcastically.

If I tell you this one little thing that happened on the train ride in, you'll know everything you need to know about Lydia. But first you have to understand that Lydia doesn't like me. Of course, she only doesn't like me on those rare occasions when she actually notices me. The rest of the time, I'm not worth not liking.

So, the four of us are sitting on the train. I'm sitting next to Mimi and across from Ari. Lydia is sitting next to the window, facing forward, because that's the best seat of the four, so of course she assumed it as her rightful throne. About twenty minutes go by. The three of us keep trying to engage Lydia in conversation. But she fans her face, says "Whatever," and continues to thumb through her fashion magazine. I go out of my way to try to pull her into a conversation. "So, it looks like bright colors are coming in," I say, pointing at the cover of her magazine.

Lydia rolls her eyes.

"You think bright colors aren't coming in?"

Lydia rolls her eyes some more.

"So what do you think the new thing in fashion is going to be?"

"Look," she says, "I'm trying to read, ok?"

In other words, it's just a typical conversation with Lydia in which she makes it clear that I am less interesting than crusted-over porridge stuck on a bowl you find behind your bed that you forgot since last winter. Not that that's ever happened to me. The point is: This is someone who really doesn't like me.

But then Mimi gets up to go to the bathroom. And as soon as she's gone, Lydia lowers the magazine from her face just enough to show her eyes. "You've got your own style, you know," she says looking straight at me.

"Me?"

"Yeah you."

"Are you kidding me? I have style? I wear the same shirt a week at a time."

"That's a style. A style is your way of showing who you are." Why did I feel like she must have just read that in her magazine? "And you show exactly who you are. You always have. Even when we were in third grade together."

Oh, I remember Lydia in the third grade all right. She was the one who took the last piece of black construction paper just because she knew that I wanted it. She cut one little circle out of the center and then "forgot" to paste it on the drawing she was making. Yeah, sure, she was admiring my style back then.

"Well, you're the first person ever to say I have anything other than a complete lack of fashion sense."

"Why do you care what other people say when you have me saying something?" And she flutters her eyelids, smiles just a bit, and goes back to reading.

Ari looks at me amazed.

I look at Ari popeyed.

She's flirting with me. Why? Because Mimi left and Lydia thinks she can and should control every boy within a thirty foot radius, even if – and this is the creepy part – she doesn't like him.

Then Mimi returned, saw Ari and me looking at each other with our eyebrows practically on top of our heads with amazement. "Later," I said to Mimi. "Later."

• • •

When we got off the train, Ari turned to the right to head uptown. "Where are you going?" Lydia demanded.

"To Mr. Sidney's," Ari said as if it were obvious.

"Mr. Sidney's" Lydia repeated as if Ari had said that he was eager to catch a case of bubonic plague. "Who goes to Mr. Sidney's?"

"That's where my..." Ari began and caught himself before admitting what we all knew: His mother takes him shopping. Just like Mimi. Just like me.

Mimi pulled Ari's sleeve towards the left. "We'll go where we usually go," she said. "The Blue Gnu."

"But we've never..."

"The Blue Gnu," Mimi repeated insistently.

"Oh," said Ari. "Yeah, the ol' Gnu. I thought you said the, um, Boo Hoo, and I'm all like, what's that, I never heard of it..."

"I can't believe you go to the Blue Gnu," said Lydia. "Actually, I totally believe it. That would explain so much," she said, looking at Ari up and down, from plaid shirt to gigantic sneakers. "We're going to La Plaz."

"La Plaz?" said Ari. "Oh, yeah, that's the other place we always go."

"Yeah. Right."

"Taxi," I shouted, and one zoomed to a stop.

La Plaz was the type of fancy shop that has a store window filled with symbols of decay. At the moment, it had a Roman Empire theme with broken columns over which were thrown sweaters so expensive that they didn't have price tags. Next to the columns were three dead indoor trees from which hung three shirts, carefully crumpled. I don't know why they think that anyone will look at that display and decide, "You know what I don't have enough of? Crumpled up shirts lying around. And not just any old crumpled shirts: I've got to get myself some really expensive ones."

We went in anyway, following Lydia, who seemed so at home there that I expected her to flop onto the floor and start doing homework...if Lydia ever actually did homework. A clerk dressed in a shirt with one short sleeve and one no-sleeve came over and pecked Lydia on both checks. "Lydia, my dear, so good to see you. Do come and take a look at what we have new for you."

"Actually, Antoine, I'm here for...him." She pointed at Ari as if he were a stain on the carpet.

"Oh. I see." Then, remembering that he was a Style Professional, Antoine turned to Ari and said in a more upbeat tone, "Why don't you come with me. My name is Antoine and I'll be working with you." Then, turning to Lydia again: "Is there an occasion?"

"He's taking Amanda to a dance at the country club."

"Oh my," said Antoine, completely failing to mask his

surprise.

Antoine whisked Ari away. Lydia followed, to pass judgment on Antoine's suggestions. It was as if she were Ari's clothing attorney, defending his rights in fashion court.

"We should be prepared for the unexpected," I said to Mimi as we browsed among racks of clothing that would look very weird on us.

"Do you think Ari is cruising for a bruising with Amanda?"

"I don't see how it could turn out well for him," I said. "There's no chance she's actually going to fall for him."

"And even if she did, that'd probably only make him more miserable."

"Yeah, not much chance of happiness coming out of this."

"So," Mimi said as she held a thing with polka dots up to her, "what were you and Ari making faces about on the train?"

"Oh, it was so weird. You know how Lydia treats me like dirt?"

"Dirt? No, that implies that she notices you."

"As soon as you left for the bathroom, she started to talk to me."

"No!"

"In fact, I'm pretty sure we actually made eye contact."

"A breakthrough!"

"But I finally figured it out. She was flirting with me."

"Really?"

"Yeah. I'm pretty sure. It was just so weird since she doesn't even like me."

"Maybe she does."

"Nah. I think it's just a natural reaction with her, like a frog sticking out its tongue to get a fly even if it's not hungry."

"I better not leave the two of you alone together."

"Help me," I said to Mimi in a high voice like the character in the movie *The Fly* – the original version, not the Jeff Goldblum version that my parents think I haven't seen because it's too gross.

Ari came toward us from the back of the store. Lydia had chased us out of there after Mimi had rolled her eyes at the puffy-sleeved green-and-pink striped shirt that Antoine had pulled out for Lydia's inspection. Ari was walking quickly and whispered in my ear: "I need more money."

"What? I gave you $500."

"The jacket and pants she's picked for me cost more than that."

"How much do you need?"

"I think it may be around $1,000 by the time she's through."

I sighed. I had the money but it seemed such a waste.

"I'm sorry," Ari said.

"Don't be. It makes zero difference," I said, handing him a wad of bills. He slipped them into his pocket, only dropping two hundreds on the way. Mimi scooped them out and gave them back to him.

"She's insane," Ari said. "She's getting me stuff that no one on the planet actually wears."

"Can we see?"

"She doesn't want you to."

"Well," said Mimi, "Tough. I'm coming back with you. We're your friends and we should be allowed at least to see. I promise not to roll my eyes again."

In the back of the store, there was a special spot for special customers. It had three comfortable chairs facing a slightly raised platform where the victim – um, customer – could stand and admire himself or herself in the three angled mirrors. Ari stepped onto the platform. I could swear that the mirrors did the fun house trick of lengthening the reflection so that you'd look just a little taller and skinnier. Clever, tricky store.

Antoine came forward carrying an arm full of ties that ranged in color from pea soup green to mold green. Apparently sickening shades of green were in this year. He began holding them up to the shirt on the top of the pile and tossed each aside with great certainty although each looked equally ugly to me. At last he came to one that looked like a muddy tire had run over an iguana. "Perfect!" he exclaimed. "And, I think you should take this one, too," he said, holding up one that looked like moss growing on a tire, "just in case the après party calls for something more festive."

Antoine looked at Lydia. Lydia looked at her watch. "Yes," said Antoine. "I believe our Mr. Ari is outfitted. Yes?" Lydia nodded. "Let me get these boxed." He waved and magically another attendant arrived who dared not look Antoine in the eye. The attendant gathered up the shirts, ties, pants, jackets, socks, underpants, undershirts, and shoes.

"Quite a load," I said as Mr. Antoine went away to total the amount and probably to order cruise tickets to celebrate the sale. "What do you think, Lydia?"

"I think he'll be well-dressed," she said, implying that that's the most Ari would ever be.

Antoine returned with two pages of bills on a small tray made out of some nearly-extinct wood. "And how will Mr. Ari pay? Credit card, may I assume?"

"No, I prefer cash," said Ari, pulling a crumpled wad of bills out of his pocket. Slowly he began counting out the amount. Bill after bill, Antoine carefully tested each to make sure that it wasn't two stuck together, then righted each so that it was face up and facing forward, then smoothed and stacked it. The hundreds, then the twenties, then the tens, then the five, then the ones. At last he was done. But, no, he began digging in his pocket for change.

"That's quite all right, Mr. Ari."

"No, I owe you thirty-two cents." So we all stood as Ari counted out five nickels and then the pennies. "I need one more," he said.

I dug in my pocket and gave him a nickel. "You owe me five cents," I said.

The three of us picked up his bundles and staggered out the door, Antoine following behind like a father sending his son to college, so proud was he. Lydia was empty-handed except for a small bag with a sweater that Antoine had given her for steering the rich Mr. Ari into the palace of fashion that was La Plaz.

The stagnant, smoggy, sooty air of the city never felt so good.

• • •

We went to lunch at Lydia's favorite restaurant, a place that had food combinations no one had ever tried before, usually for good reason. It was just a block past the Salzburg Grille where we had had lunch the last time we were in the city. As we approached, all three of us looked to see Philip and Caroline.

Their spot was empty. Even the rags where Spunky had slept were gone.

Chapter 17

I was now reading both *The Gazette* and *The Register* especially carefully. I took both upstairs as soon as they arrived and went through them article by article. I wasn't only looking at which advertisers were sticking with my father. I was also checking to see who was in trouble and might benefit from a grant from the Fordgythe Foundation. And there were lots of candidates.

For example, the animal shelter was overstuffed and under-funded. They'd gone to the Town Council to get emergency money because they were out of room for stray animals, but the Town Council voted to give them only half of the money they needed, a measly $5,000. The poor little doggies looked so cute and sad in the photo the paper ran. The cats would have looked cute and sad if I cared about cats. I left that job to Mimi.

Then there was the Burnish Bob project. Some citizens were distressed that the big statue of Robert Melville in the triangular park at the center of town was black, green and white instead of the bright bronze it started out as. Some people had started a petition to get the statue scrubbed and restored, especially the white part which was, well, pigeon poop. Yes, apparently Robert Melville, founder of our town and the maker of fine cannons during the War of 1812, was also our pigeon population's most appealing public restroom. Heck, sometimes I was tempted myself to ... well, never mind.

I can't say that the Burnish Bob project mattered very much

to me. I'd let Bob wear his coat of white proudly if the money could instead go to help those cutey-wootey widdle puppies. Not that I'd ever talk that way.

I went ahead and dropped off a bundle of money at the animal shelter, neatly tied with my mother's yarn and with a note on my expensive Fordgythe paper. But I couldn't decide what to do about the stupid statue problem. It's not a project I cared about, but apparently it meant a lot to other people. So why should I spend my money on it? Because, no matter how dumb it seemed to me, polishing Bob would make a bunch of people happier. Besides, in the time I spent thinking about it, I'd practically earned enough interest to pay for it. So, Bob got his $6,500.

But there were more projects just waiting to be pushed along. I contributed $30,000 to a scholarship fund so that the Corner Coop Pre-School could take in kids whose parents couldn't afford to send them. Maddie had gone there when she was four and I'd always enjoyed going with my mother to pick her up because the library paste smelled so good. Also, Rachel the teacher was so enthusiastic about "opening up the minds of young people."

And I read about an immigrant from Honduras who was going to be sent back because she didn't fill in a form right even though she was taking care of her sick brother. So, I mailed her $10,000 so she could get a good lawyer and also get some help for her brother. I had no idea if that was enough or too much, but it seemed like a reasonable guess.

And then there was the School Summer Gala. It was on the verge of being cancelled. This was big enough news to make it onto the front page, although I didn't notice it at first because the cutey-wootey-kazootie picture of the widdle-biddle puppy-wuppies distracted me.

The Summer Gala was a big deal. Every year, on the weekend that school ended, there'd be a huge picnic in the afternoon followed by an evening party for all grades, parents invited. And this wasn't just a spread-out-a-tablecloth sort of picnic. This was free food and soda, pony rides, a magician wandering around, a dunk-the-teachers booth, and a cake big enough to feed the entire school with enough left over for throwing.

Normally the money was provided by local businesses who kicked into the school's Activities Funds in return for a mention in the year book and a small sign strung up on the fence behind the basketball court where the beverages were served. This year, though, there'd been a big drop in contributions, probably because the whole town was going through a hard time when it came to money.

I, of course, was having a fabulously good year when it came to money. So the Summer Gala got the money it needed from a source it wasn't expecting and had never heard of.

• • •

That night was the country club dance. I'd arranged for a limo to pick up Ari. But first it picked up me and Mimi a few blocks from Mimi's house. From there the limo driver – a college student who was making some money on the weekends – went to pick up Ari in his new clothes. The driver let Mimi and me off at the country club and then went to pick up Amanda.

The country club was set back from the road a long way. Of course the lawn on either side of the road leading up to it was perfectly manicured. Of course attendants in silly uniforms opened the doors of the elegant cars for the elegant people inside. Of course the big gates were kept locked. Mimi and I sat halfway up the lawn, behind one of the few bushes.

"I bet he tugs on his underwear when he gets out of the car," I said.

"No. Not even Ari would do that."

"He does it every time he gets up from a seat. He's got a permanent wedgie."

We didn't have to wait long to find out. The big, black limo pulled up. I knew it was Ari's because the license plate was "HERNITE" which I at first thought was the name of some mineral but then I figured out it was actually supposed to be read as "her nite" as in "her nite out." It came to a slow stop at the top of the gravel driveway. Immediately the attendants swarmed around it as if opening the car door were a matter of national urgency. Out poked the long legs of Amanda looking splendid in an organdy chenille dress. (Mimi told me what it was later.) And then came Ari, new shoes first, then carefully pressed new pants, followed by the complete Ari, looking pretty sharp. If you didn't know it was Ari, you'd say he was a good dresser. The feet hit the ground, Ari shook his shoulders to straighten his coat, shot his arms forward to get them out of the cuffs, reached behind to his butt...and took out his wallet to tip the attendant.

"Cool move!" I said.

"You were totally wrong, mister."

"And never happier to be so."

As Ari replaced the wallet, I could see that he was secretly working on removing the wedgie. But it was subtle, almost slick. The boy was going to be ok.

Mimi and I sat for a moment more, listening to the sound of the band drifting over the wall. Then we took a long walk to my house so she could kick my butt in video games.

Three hours later, Ari was knocking on our door. The knock alarmed my parents, but when my mother saw it was Ari, she only said "Eleven's a little late, don't you think, Ari?" But as Mimi and I flew down the stairs to meet him, I said to them, "Girl trouble. He wants to talk." That probably alarmed them even more.

The three of us sat on the swing set in my yard. Ari didn't speak. He didn't swing. He just smiled.

"So, Ari, spill your guts!" I said.

"Yeah," chimed in Mimi, "So what happened at your big dinner-dance date with the rich folk." Then, remembering the size of my bank account, Mimi turned to me and said, "You're not really a rich person. You've just got a lot of money."

"Oh," said Ari, coming back to the planet earth, "it was terrible. So bad it was funny."

"Oh no! But was Amanda at least everything you hoped for?"

"Amanda?" he said, as if he were unfamiliar with the name, "She's an idiot."

"She dumped you?"

"Dumped me? No. She was never going with me. It turns out I was just a practical joke Lydia was playing on Amanda because after Amanda broke up with Roger, Amanda wouldn't let Lydia go out with him. I was a revenge date."

"That must have been so embarrassing!" said Mimi.

"No," said Ari, surprised at the suggestion. "Well, if Amanda weren't an idiot maybe it would have been. But it's like getting rejected by a… a…"

"A garden gnome?" Mimi suggested.

"A fur ball?" I suggested.

"No, it's like being rejected by this incredibly shallow, conceited, empty-headed…"

"Nasty…" Mimi added.

"Manipulative…" I added.

"Idiot," Ari finished.

We sat silently contemplating what had happened: Ari had come to his senses. And I hadn't known he even had senses to come to.

Mimi squeezed has hand. "She's an idiot. You're definitely not."

Ari shook his head slightly, not convinced.

The moon poked out from behind the clouds, seeming to

remind Ari of what he came over to tell us.

"But something really cool happened. I was sitting at Mr. Dunn's table ..."

"You were sitting at his table? You?"

"Yeah. He saw what was happening and I think he felt bad for me. So he called me over and I sat at his table for most of the night. He's really not such a bad guy. I mean, it's like he's from another planet with how he treats people and what he worries about, but on his planet he's probably considered a heck of a nice guy."

"I doubt it."

"No, it's true. He let me sit there all night so I wouldn't have to deal with his idiot daughter. Anyway, he talked with me a little, about sports and why being a financial analyst would be a good career for me, but mainly I just sat there listening to what he was talking about with everyone who came by. And everyone did come by. He knows everyone."

"Well, everyone who goes to a country club dinner dance."

"Anyway, he was talking with some guy in a tuxedo about the Fordgythe Foundation."

"No!"

"Yes he was."

"What did he say?"

"Someone asked him if he'd heard about this new foundation that's been dropping cash around, and he said he had, but I

190

think he was just trying to sound smart."

"Who was the guy who was talking with him?" I asked.

"I don't know. Just a guy. Friendly with him. Anyhoo, Mr. Dunn asked the guy if he had any details. But the guy said just that it was always cash, and that the stationery looked phony."

"Not at all, dear," said Mimi, comforting me. But we both knew that the guy – whoever that guy was – was right. I'm not a grown up, professional designer, and I'm not ashamed to admit it. Much.

"Anyhoo…" I prompted.

"That's about it. Except Mr. Dunn said that he had someone at *The Register* looking into it."

"Well, if he didn't before, he does now."

"Should we be worried?" Ari asked.

"Not until we do something wrong."

But I was worried a little. I didn't want anyone to find out who was behind the Fordgythe Institute's money. And I didn't want *The Register* to scoop my own father's paper.

• • •

I needn't have worried. The very next day when I came down to watch TV in the study, my father was on the phone, standing in his journalism pose. You know how when you're in a crowd you turn your head if you hear your name mentioned even though you weren't listening to the person who said it? I wasn't paying attention to my father's conversation until I heard him say, "Foundation?"

"Yes, definitely. Very interesting. I'll check into it. Thanks for the tip."

When he'd hung up, I said – all casual-like – "Who was that?"

"A source." Obviously he wasn't going to tell me who.

"Hot tip?

"Could be. An interesting story. It seems that some foundation no one ever heard of has been giving people money."

"Don't foundations do that all the time?"

"Yes, sure. But not cash. And not to people who haven't applied for a grant."

"Interesting."

"I'm going to look into it."

"If you need any help…" I began.

"Yes?"

"Well, I'm sure you can get whatever help you need."

I turned back to the TV. But I wasn't really watching. I was thinking about whether I had covered my tracks well enough.

Chapter 18

That afternoon, we prepared more bundles of cash. Twenty in all, each wrapped in my Mom's yarn. Each recipient had been researched on line. Each was needy and worthy. I felt good about what we were about to do. There was one big difference from the previous donations: eighteen of the twenty were in the city because I didn't want to get caught by either of the two local papers investigating my Foundation. We printed up the notices, tucked one into each bundle, and set off for the train station, the bundles in a brown bag in my backpack.

"Um, you might want to zip that thing," Mimi said as I was getting on my bike. She leaned over and zipped my backpack for me. "We don't want to get there and find out that $80,000 was lying in a brown paper bag by the side of the road somewhere."

"No. But you know what the scary thing is?"

She nodded.

"It'd just be a bother to go down to the bank again," I said.

We had a tight schedule in the city: Eighteen places to go and just a few hours to do it in if we were to make it back in time for dinner.

Most of the bundles, plain white envelopes with labels printed out from my computer, were easy to deliver. We could have taken a single cab, leapt out, and continued to the next stop, but we didn't want the cabby to figure out that we were the ones leaving the little bundles of joy. So, we'd go uptown to the address of a health clinic that we'd read was on the verge of closing, we'd leave the envelope in its mail box, and either walk to the next spot or take a cab. An A student who couldn't afford college, a veteran's club that was raising money for a new roof, a little something for a woman who spent her weekends doing puppet shows in the children's hospital – they all got their envelopes, as did another ten people or organizations.

That left five more bundles for the city. It didn't take long to find five people living on the streets. We'd listen to them and then look at one another. If we all agreed, we'd give them an envelope. "You can probably use this. It's completely legal. Just spend it well, ok?" And then we'd leave before they could open it.

The truth is, I still wasn't sure that that was a good way to spend the money. I knew the argument that they'll just spend it on alcohol or drugs. But I'll tell you the part of the argument that I didn't like: the "they" part. They weren't "they." They're people, each different. And some might use the money to get drunk for months. But maybe they wouldn't. I don't know that even "they" know ahead of time what the effect of $1,000 in cash would be.

We made it back just before our parents would be getting annoyed at us. I asked my parents if I could go out for another twenty minutes. That gave me just enough time to drop off the last two bundles. A veteran and a synagogue were going to have a better day than they thought they were going to have.

On the way back, I put an envelope in the mail. It was

addressed to my father and inside was a message from the Fordgythe Foundation. I used a font I'd downloaded especially so that Dad wouldn't recognize it as having coming from my computer. It was an ugly font, but better ugly than recognizable. I figured my father would get the letter the next day.

• • •

The next night when we sat down to dinner, my father couldn't wait to tell us his news. He was so excited that he started buttering a second roll before he realized he hadn't eaten the first. "You'll never guess what happened," he said. I tried not to blurt out: "You received a mysterious letter in the mail!"

"I got a phone call," he said.

Odd, I thought. I was quite sure I had mailed him a letter and not phoned him. I mentally reviewed the difference between a mailbox and a phone booth. Yup, I had definitely sent him mail.

"The debate over the lottery is set. It's in three weeks."

"That's wonderful," said my mother. "Did they send you a contract?"

My mother's father was a lawyer and taught her not to believe anything is going to happen unless there's a signed contract. That's why she doesn't believe weather reporters on TV. "They can say whatever they want and there's no accountability." Accountability means that if you're wrong about the weather, you get punished. My mother would like weathermen to get paid according to how many right predictions they make.

"Not yet," my father said, "but the show is on their schedule. And do you know who I'm going to be debating?"

We waited.

"Geoffrey Dunn." Amanda's father. Mr. Dunn.

"That's so exciting," my mother said. "That will get more viewers." Mr. Dunn was well known around the state.

"I can't wait to start preparing."

"You're already well-prepared," my mother said. "You've been researching this for years."

"I know, but I want to have arguments that really work. And I want to anticipate the arguments that Mr. Dunn will use."

"Lotteries are good because it's good to be rich," I suggested in a voice that was a truly lousy imitation of Mr. Dunn's.

"But is it better to make one person very rich at the expense of many people who can't afford it? Isn't the lottery really a tax on the poor?" My father was speaking in his Public Speaking voice, louder and smoother than his real voice.

"But it's a so-called tax that they choose to pay because they get some enjoyment from it," I said as Mr. Dunn. "Shouldn't they be allowed to choose how they get their enjoyment?"

"They get enjoyment from it because the state tells them that they have a chance of winning."

"But they do have a chance of winning. The same chance as everyone else. And it says the chance right on the back of the lottery ticket."

"In tiny print," my father said, "while meanwhile the state

is buying posters and billboards with very big print to convince people that they're just one ticket away from being rich."

"So, you don't trust the citizens of this fair state," I said Dunn-ishly, "to make their own choices. You think citizens are so easily fooled. You think we're stupid stupid sheep…"

"You know," my father said not in his public voice, "that's the hardest argument to fight. I look like an elitist."

"A what-ist?"

"Someone who thinks he's better than everyone else. Someone who thinks those poor people are just too dumb to know what's good for them."

"But isn't that what you're saying?" my mother asked, surprising me.

"I'm saying that I believe in the power of advertising. It works. So, now the state government is advertising how the lottery will make you rich and end all your worries. Everyone can be fooled by advertising. That's why companies spend millions and millions of dollars doing it to sell you stuff you didn't originally want."

"So, it's not the lottery you disagree with, but the advertising for it," I said as Mr. Dunn again.

"Hmm," my father said. "Take away the advertising and the lottery is just a bad gamble that will take money from the poorest of us – because studies show that poorer areas play lotteries more than richer areas."

"But, the money goes to education," I said.

"The education budget – which, by the way, I'd like to see

enlarged – should be paid for like every other service the state government provides," my father replied.

"So," my mother said, doing an even worse imitation of Mr. Dunn, "you'd like to see a tax increase on all of us to make up for the money we're raising for education through the lottery?"

"I'd like to see all the money we need for education given to education without having to rely on tricking people into buying lottery tickets. You don't get anything for free, and if we have to raise taxes a little to pay for education, then, yes, we ought to be willing to do that."

I said, "You should add: '...for the children.' That always seems to work."

"For the children," my father said and laughed. "I'll try to work that phrase in as much as possible."

"Can't go wrong," I said.

• • •

I checked the Fordgythe Foundation's email address every ten minutes the next day. At last, at 5:30 there was a message from my father:

Dear Anonymous,

I received your letter with your offer to give The Gazette an exclusive email interview with the head of the Fordgythe Foundation.

Unfortunately, I must decline this offer. It is the policy of The

Gazette not to engage in interviews
solely through email since with
email we can't guarantee our readers
that we are interviewing the person
we think we're interviewing.

If you would like to arrange to meet
in person, I would be delighted to
set up an appointment.

Thank you.

PS: That is one ugly font you used
in your letter! ☺

So much for that plan for getting more people to read *The Gaz*. If only my father were a little sleazier!

Chapter 19

We had a plan that I thought was pretty good. I just didn't expect it to be so completely interrupted by a pancake breakfast. But then, the town Fireman's Pancake Breakfast is always at least a little surprising.

It's something our town does to raise money for extra activities that our taxes don't pay for. I've been going ever since I was a tadpole because my father, as the editor of the town's best newspaper, is always invited and sits at the table at the head of the room. Oh, and gets pancake syrup poured on him. Every year. They call it a tradition, but I think it's just plain hilarious.

My father says it began before I was born when he threw a pancake Frisbee-style at Alderman Byrd. Alderman Byrd threw it back, but missed. So he got up slowly and carefully, and poured an entire pitcher of maple syrup over my father's head.

As I said, hilarious.

It turned into a tradition the next year when my father made the mistake of showing up in a raincoat and rain hat, the sort that salty old seamen wear. Alderman Byrd took this as a challenge. The next year my father brought an umbrella. And after that, he gave up trying to protect himself. He shows up in a shirt he doesn't care too much about and sits there silently as Alderman Byrd syrups him.

This year, the money raised by the breakfast was going to a cause that Mimi cared about a lot. The Tulip Time Nursery.

It's a daycare center that the town funds for families that can't afford the more expensive ones. Mimi volunteers there during the summer and goes on some of their class trips. Over the past few years, the town had given the Tulip Troop, as the kids were known, less and less money because there wasn't much money to give out. The nursery raised some money through donations and bake sales. They even sold the tiny little tomatoes and half-grown cucumbers that the Troop spent all summer growing. I'd pass by the garden sometimes, and the sight of those little kids whacking at the ground with their plastic hoes as if they were actually gardening was maybe the cutest thing I'd ever seen.

So, when Alderman Byrd asked Mimi to help put up signs advertising the Pancake Breakfast, she was torn. On the one hand, she wanted to raise money for the Tulip Troop, what with them being so cute and all. On the other hand, she thought Alderman Byrd was going too far: The signs showed a big, juicy photo of my father looking calmly into the camera as syrup dripped over his head and down off his glasses. The fact that you also got to eat pancakes at the breakfast was hardly even mentioned.

Mimi showed me a copy of the flyer. "Don't worry about it," I said to her. "It'll probably draw a lot of people, and that's what everyone wants. Even my father."

But it gave me an idea that required me to hire my very first employee. I needed an adult who could buy some things without anyone getting suspicious. "That's a great idea," Mimi said. "There are so many things that'd be easier if we had a grown up to do them for us." Even something as simple as getting business cards printed up is tough for a kid to do without making people suspicious.

But who? One of our teachers? No, that would make going to school too complicated because we'd always have to pretend that nothing was going on. Besides, I'm not sure it's legal for students to hire their teachers. One of my relatives? No, they might let the secret slip to my parents. Mr. Seoul, the guy who drives the ice cream truck? He seemed like a really nice guy, but I'm not sure I'd trust with him a $100,000,000 secret.

Then it came to me. Remember Julia Minden, the teller at the bank where all my money is? Probably not since I only mentioned her once and that was a long time ago. Ms. Minden was about twenty-five years old, tall, and had the sort of smile that is so bright it makes you want to duck. Every time I'd gone into the bank, we'd chatted a little. I really liked her. Not only was she helpful and cheerful, but she didn't treat me like a little rich kid. Plus, she was already in on the secret. Mimi and I went to see her.

"Hello, Jake," she said, like someone genuinely pleased to see me.

"Hello. Do you know my friend Mimi?"

"You've been in with your mother. How is your father doing, Mimi?"

"Good," Mimi said.

"Can we talk with you privately about something?" I asked.

"Of course." She caught the eye of Ms. Harrigan who waved to her that it was ok to take a little break, seeing that it was with me. Ah, the privileges having money gives you!

We went into one of the bank's private rooms and I laid out the deal: "We're looking for a grownup to help us, and we're wondering if you'd be interested."

"Help you do what?"

"Help us do the things that we're doing with our money," I said.

"It's not really *our* money," Mimi said to me. "It's yours."

"Well, yes," I said.

"But we're not doing anything evil with it," Mimi said. "There are just some things that it's really tough for kids to do."

"Especially if no one is supposed to know that they have money," I added.

Ms. Minden sat thinking,

"We'd pay you," I said. I'd somehow left that part out.

"Would I keep my job here at the bank?"

"Yes. We would only need you to do things every now and then."

She looked at me now like someone who had made up her mind. "I trust you. And I like what you've been doing with the Fordgythe Foundation."

"You know about that?"

"It wasn't hard to figure out since Mrs. Fordgythe is the one who transferred the money to you."

"So you'll do it?"

"I'd be happy to."

"Great!" We sat for a moment. "How much do we pay you?"

She laughed, "I don't know."

"How can you not know? You're a grownup!"

"But salaries don't work that way. Usually you're not paid much more or less than other people in the company doing the same job with the same amount of experience. But this isn't like that. So, we just have to figure something out."

"Well," I said, "It doesn't matter much to me because I have so much money."

"Yes, I have that going in my favor," she said, laughing again. "But we're just going to have to come up with an amount we both think is right."

So here's what happened in the negotiation. She began with an amount that was about a tenth of what she made as a bank teller. By the time we were done bargaining, I had gotten her to accept a salary of half as much as she made. She thought I was terribly overpaying her and I thought I was terribly underpaying her. I guess you could call that a successful compromise.

Now that Ms. Minden worked for me, I told her my plan. She laughed and asked how she could help.

There was only one thing left for me and Mimi to do: Download a picture of Big Bird. By the next morning we'd posted 100 flyers around town. "Big Byrd invites you to the

Pancake Breakfast to benefit the Tulip Time Nursery," said. And in the center was a photo of Big Bird with Alderman Byrd's face imposed on it. Sometimes I love computers.

I knew that some people called him Big Byrd because he was shaped roughly like that overgrown chicken on *Sesame Street*. In fact, I once saw him in shorts in the park and his legs were as thin and knobby as Big Bird's. The Alderman didn't like the comparison at all. Not even a little bit. So we figured we'd annoy him before the big day. Why not? It was for a good cause.

The day before the breakfast, Ms. Minden sent me an email saying that everything was all arranged. When I asked who had built the stuff we needed, I was surprised to find out that it was Mr. Paul, the Dunns' butler and handyman. "I had to tell him what it was for," Ms. Minden wrote back to me. "I didn't want him to think it was for something illegal."

"You trust him enough for that?" I replied.

"Actually, yes. Of course I didn't mention your name or anything about winning the lottery. I just said I was doing some odd jobs for an eccentric rich person. But I've known Mr. Paul for a while. We're in a book club. He's very honest. And he has a great sense of humor."

Wow. The things you learn about someone in a book club!

The night before the breakfast, my father was laying out the clothes he was going to wear. Alderman Byrd traditionally poured carefully onto the top part of my father's head so that the syrup could flow all down my father's face. And from the face it went to the collar and from there on down until by the time my father got up, he left a syrup mark on the seat. Gross, when you think about it, which I try not to do. So, the clothes he wore had to be disposable, but also nice enough that it didn't look like he was dressing for the syruping that was bound to happen.

I looked at the checked shirt and the black jeans. "Nice," I said. "Going a little informal this year?"

"Yes," he said jokingly, "It's only a breakfast. No need to get all dressed up."

"Yeah, sure. I mean, suppose you spilled some, I don't know, syrup on yourself. You wouldn't want to get your good clothes all sticky."

"Spill syrup? Why, what are the chances of that?" he said and laughed. He picked out a pair of nice fuzzy socks.

"Wouldn't it be nice if Alderman Byrd got syruped one year instead of you?" I asked.

"Ol' Big Byrd? I wouldn't say no. But it's a tradition. I don't mind it. In fact, it's even sort of an honor."

"An honor?"

"Sure." my father said, running his hand through what used to be his hair. "They wouldn't do this to someone they didn't know and like." Then he looked at me, panicked: "Would they?"

He was kidding.

"I'll wake you at eight tomorrow," Dad said.

"I'll probably be awake by then," I said. I'd better be. I had work to do.

• • •

The breakfast began at nine o'clock, but the only ones who got there that early were either town officials like Big Byrd or those who really wanted to get their money's worth of the as-many-as-you-can-eat pancake offer. My father, as a town notable, showed up shortly after nine. Mimi was already there because she didn't want to miss a minute of it. And in the front of the room at the table closest to where the volunteers were serving the pancakes was Ari, already on his third plate.

We hadn't told Ari our plans. Mimi had asked about that a couple of days earlier. "Why don't we not," I suggested. "That way he can be surprised by what happens."

"Yeah, it'll be more fun for him."

In truth, though, I think something else was going on. I think Mimi and I wanted to have something that was only ours. That may not have been the nicest thing to do to our friend Ari, but we had a good excuse…good for him and good for ourselves.

Mimi was watching for me. "Is everything…?" she started to ask as she came towards me.

"It's all done," I said. It had been done by six am. Which meant that we'd started it at five am. Even though it was almost summer, at that time in the morning it was chilly. I'd met Mr. Paul behind the building. He was drinking coffee from an insulated cup. It smelled good, and I don't like coffee. So I was very pleased when Mr. Paul reached into his bag and pulled out a thermos filled with hot chocolate and an empty mug for me. I guess being a butler teaches you how to be considerate. "Are you ready?" he asked me?

I nodded. "Did you bring everything?"

He pointed at the duffel bag next to him.

So we entered the pancake house through a window and did what we planned on doing.

"Phase 2 went according to plan," I said to Mimi.

"Phase 2? What was Phase 1?"

"You know, figuring stuff out."

We got good seats towards the front, but out of spray range, and chowed down on some pretty good pancakes.

The speeches didn't begin until 10:30, and they were short because everyone knew that we weren't there to hear local politicians drone on and on about how proud they were to support this and oppose that and how pleased they were to vote for giving the firefighters new red suspenders. The people in the room were there for two reasons and two reasons only: to eat pancakes and to watch my dad get syruped. Every speech only postponed the time when my father would be drenched in sticky, icky, gooey goo.

My father was doing his usual thing, pretending that he didn't know anything was going to happen to him, listening to the speeches as if he were actually interested instead of wondering just when Selectman Byrd would be coming over with that big pitcher of maple syrup.

As usual, Selectman Byrd was waiting for the end of the

speeches because as soon as he did the deed, no one would even pretend to listen to the rest of them. The fifth town official was finishing up. She was explaining how proud she was to support the library's new library cards, the ones with a lovely picture of Melvil Dewey on them – he apparently was the inventor of the Dewey Decimal System – and there didn't seem to be any town officials left. It was just as she was expressing her admiration not only for Dewey but for decimals – where would we be without them? – that Selectman Byrd rose from his seat. Quietly. No big fuss. But everyone was watching him, as he well knew.

Now pretending to whistle casually, he was approaching my father from behind. Dad was putting the last bite of pancakes into his mouth, rolling his eyes, pretending to be enjoying them as much as if they were a fancy dessert at the country's best restaurant.

Up creeps Selectman Byrd. And now from behind his back he brings the pitcher of syrup. Except this time it's not a pitcher. It's one of those gigantic water pistols, the type that hold a gallon. The Selectman is pumping it up with air so that he'll get a good stream out of it. My father must be able to hear him, but he acts as if nothing is going on behind him. People are giggling. All eyes are on the Selectman.

And watching the closest are me and Mimi because everything depends on Selectman Byrd standing right behind my father. The water pistol means he'll stand too far away. Mimi looks at me. I look at her.

Slowly, Selectman Byrd comes forward. Ten feet away. Eight feet away. Five feet away.

And he fires.

A stream of syrup hits my father in the back of the head and drips down his collar.

The Selectman gets a nice arc in the stream so that it drops down on him like a slow shower.

My father slowly turns to face him, as if wondering what's going on. The Selectman hoses him in the face.

Five feet away, in the wrong place. And there's nothing Mimi or I can do.

Then, as the syrup continues to stream down his face, my father reaches under the table. He has two cans of whipped cream taped there. He stands up. He aims them both at the Selectman.

Pay back.

The Selectman pumps up his water gun again but the stream stays weak.

My father steps backwards.

The Selectman steps forward. Five feet from where my father had been sitting. Three feet. One foot.

I press the button on the device in my pocket.

It sends a radio signal to the devices Mr. Paul installed in the ceiling. The signal releases magnets that were holding the latches closed.

From the ceiling comes five gallons of butterscotch sauce, the only thing we could think of that was stickier than maple syrup.

Selectman Byrd is stopped in his tracks. He is stunned. He stands there, his arms at his sides, as the butterscotch sauce trickles down his head, down his shirt, into his pants.

Butterscotch sauce is coming out of the cuffs of his pants.

And then I press the second button.

Do you know how many fake yellow feathers there are in two pounds? More than enough to cover an entire large Selectman who has been recently coated with butterscotch sauce.

Big Byrd stood there flapping his wings as if he were really Big Bird.

And I thought to myself: For a waste of money, it was worth every penny.

Chapter 20

I found it both annoying and typical of my father that he didn't run a photo of the Big Birding of Selectman Byrd in *The Gaz*. He said that he didn't feel it was "appropriate" for his newspaper to run a picture that would embarrass someone, especially since it might be seen as my father trying to get back at him.

I guess I understand that. Even so, I had been looking forward to seeing the photo smack dab in the middle of the front page.

The Register ran it on the front page. To make matters worse, the caption said the newspaper was "investigating the mastermind behind the stunt." I guess that would be me. And since *The Register* was also investigating The Fordgythe Foundation, I must have been #1 on their Most Wanted List, although they of course didn't know that.

Then there was the lottery debate. It was coming up soon. My father was getting more and more nervous about it. He had been collecting information for months. Now he was muttering to himself possible questions and answers, correcting himself to himself, and then restating the answer to himself.

Finally, one more event was driving my father crazy. At the center of the latest issue of *The Register* were 16 pages of ads, all from the Red Mount "You Want It, We Got It" MultiStore. And on every page, advertising everything from tents to French pastry, there was a big, colorful coupon: "Take an extra 10% off." That's the type of ad that gets people to buy newspapers.

Or so said my father, as he muttered and sputtered.

In fact, my kind, gentle, caring, loving father had actually yelled at me. He never yelled, much less over something like leaving my breakfast dishes on the table. In fact, he didn't really yell this time, if by "yell" you mean "make your voice get loud." But he said, "Clear your dishes" with a tone that wasn't kind, gentle or caring. Sort of stern, the way the captain of a ship might say, "I told you once before, you point the cannon *away* from the ship." Something like that. But, in any case, it wasn't like my father. He was feeling the pressure.

Ari, Mimi and I sat in my room and played a video game that I'd bought for Ari and he'd thoughtfully brought with him. Both he and Mimi were kicking my butt. I might as well have been playing while trying to get into my good sports jacket which was two sizes too small and completely out of fashion anyway. Still, the only time I ever wore it was to Grown Up events where it really doesn't matter what you look like anyway. Not that this has anything to do with how badly I was playing.

"What can we do?" asked Ari, adding another 500 points to his score.

"About the advertising? I don't know."

"I hate that Red Mount store," Mimi said. "It's too big. If you're in sporting goods and remember that you forgot to pick up toothpaste, it's like a four mile march back."

"And then you remember that you forgot pine scented room deodorant," said Ari. We looked at him. If you'd ever been in Ari's room, you'd know why he was looking for room deodorizer.

"We could pay people not to go there," Mimi said, knowing as she said it that it wasn't a very good idea.

"We could phone in skunk reports," Ari said. "You know, we call the police and tell them that we've seen skunks there. They'd clear the building and..."

"Ari," I said, "I don't think they clear buildings when someone reports a skunk sighting."

"Well, they ought to."

Ari was now approximately a bazillion points ahead of me in the video game.

"We could offer Red Mount the same deal as Mr. Dunn did and get them to advertise in *The Gaz*," Mimi suggested.

"My dad says that Red Mount's contract probably says they'll only advertise in *The Register*."

"So, do you have a better idea?" Mimi asked. She must have been feeling the pressure, too.

"No, not really. I'd just rather do something positive to get more people advertising in *The Gaz* instead of skunking *The Register*, if you know what I mean."

"I thought you said skunking wasn't a good idea," Ari said.

"It was just a figure of speech."

"Why not do the same thing for some other store," Ari said as the video game clanged another 1,000 points onto his score. "You know, like the Game Dungeon."

"You know," said Mimi, "that's not such a bad idea."

"Yeah," said Ari, "The Game Dungeon is such a great store."

"But not just for the Game Dungeon," Mimi continued. "For all the local stores."

"All of them?"

"All of them that advertise in *The Gaz*."

"I like it," I said. "It's positive and it's local. But I'm not sure it's quite right."

"Why not?"

"I don't know. I'm just not sure it's going to work."

"Then how about beating the 10% discount *The Register* is giving," Mimi said. "Interesting," I said, "but why would the Fordgythe Foundation want to make it cheaper for you to buy asparagus and toilet paper?"

"Because they make such a delicious salad together?" Mimi suggested.

I was doing the last of my homework that night when I had an idea. It could work, but only if Ms. Minden helped.

I went to see her after school on Monday. As I parked my bike in the alley beside the bank because I didn't want people to notice how much time I was spending there, I thought I saw someone duck out of the way, as if he didn't want me to see him. Out of the corner of my eye, I saw dark pants, white sneakers, and what looked like antennae coming out of his head. It must have been my imagination, I told myself.

Inside, Julia took me into a private office and I told her

our plan.

"Cool!" she said. "But it's going to be a little tricky to arrange."

"I know."

"I think I know what to do. Just leave it to me."

"No one can know it's coming from me."

"Of course. The money is going to come from the Fordgythe Foundation, naturally."

"It should happen pretty quickly. *The Gaz* can't survive too long if it doesn't have advertisers…"

"I understand. Let me draw up a plan and give it to you."

I liked the sound of that. Mimi, Ari and I hadn't drawn up plans. We'd just had ideas and done stuff. Julia was really working out.

So, I was feeling better when I came home that afternoon. But that didn't last long. When I walked in, my father was pacing the living room floor, reading out loud from some pages he'd printed, and my mother was sitting in a chair.

My mother said, "No, no, I don't think you should say that playing the lottery is like throwing your money away, because to the people who play the lottery, it doesn't feel like that at all. They think they're buying a chance to win millions of dollars, not throwing their money away."

"But they have no chance of winning!" my father said.

"But they do have a chance. A tiny chance, but a chance."

"But it's not a chance worth spending money on."

"No, of course not. But the people who play the lottery think they're buying a small chance so when you say that they're not buying any chance, they're going to stop listening to you."

"I'm not going to lie to them and tell them that they're buying something worthwhile when they buy a lottery ticket."

"Of course not," my mother said patiently. "I'm not saying you should. But you're telling them that there's *no* chance of winning, but there really is a chance, it's just a tiny tiny tiny chance. You're not talking from their point of view and so they won't listen to you."

"I don't want to talk from their point of view because their point of view is ridiculous," my father said.

"And if that's your attitude – that the million people who buy a lottery ticket every week are stupid and ridiculous – then you're never going to get listened to. You don't have to agree with them to talk to them from their point of view. You know that. That's why you're such a good writer."

"I don't even know what you're saying any more," my father said. "You want me to speak from their point of view but not speak from their point of view, and tell them they have a chance to win the lottery when they don't…"

"I actually haven't said any of those things," my mother said, forcing herself to be patient. "But I think maybe this isn't such a good time for me to listen to what you plan on saying. Maybe in a day or two."

"Fine, if you don't want to help me…"

"You know that's not true. Let's just do this later." And with that, my mother left the living room.

My dad really isn't the jerk who was practicing for the debate. It was as if an alien jerk had invaded his body. I guess nervousness will do that to you.

My father was still pacing, scratching at the printout he had been reading from. I went upstairs and did my homework.

The next morning, as I rode to school, I noticed Julia in her car, waving to me. I pulled up next to her.

"Here it is," she said, handing me an envelope.

"Excellent!" I said, tucking it carefully it into my backpack.

She drove away. And I thought I saw someone with antennae coming out of his head duck into the garage across the street.

It must have been my imagination.

But of course it wasn't.

Chapter 21

"Why are you following me?" I asked the space alien behind me.

"Huh?" he asked, if "Huh" can really count as a question.

"You've been following me. I want to know why." I sounded brave but my knees were weak. Fortunately, it was a sunny day on a busy street or I wouldn't have had the nerve to confront the guy with the antennas.

Of course, it helped that he was no alien. The antennas were pencils, one behind each ear.

"I haven't been following you," he said.

"Then how come every time I turn around, I see you scurrying out of the way?"

"I'm not scurrying…"

"Aha! Then you admit that you've been following me!"

"No. How do you get that?"

"Because you said you weren't scurrying, but didn't deny that you were following me."

"That's because you cut me off with your 'Aha!' If you'd let me finish, I would have denied the whole thing." He looked like he'd just graduated high school. In fact, I thought I recognized him from around town.

"So, you deny that you've been following me."

"Yes, that's what I've been denying for the past ten

minutes."

"Really?" I was beginning to feel pretty stupid. "Because I was pretty sure it was you that's been following me. Someone has been. At least I think so."

"Yeah, well, it was me."

"Really?"

"Yeah."

"So why were you denying it before?"

"Wouldn't you? I mean, that's part of following someone around. When they catch you, you deny it."

"But you're admitting it now."

"Yeah," he said, pulling one of the pencils from behind his ear. "I mean, you've caught me at it. I'm not going to be able to follow you any more. So, I might as well admit it."

"Wow! I really did catch you!"

"Yes," he said, "But it's a little embarrassing. Would you mind not telling anyone you caught me at it? After all, I admitted it when I could have kept on denying it."

"Well, I guess that's fair. But you have to tell me why you're following me."

"Sure. I was going to anyway."

I waited. I was holding my bike up. We were about a block from the bank. "So?"

"Ok," he said, pulling a pad from his back pocket. "I work for *The Register.*"

"No!" I didn't like where this was going.

"Actually I work for Mr. Dunn."

It was getting worse. "What's he interested in me for?" Because my father owned the town's other newspaper? Because Mr. Dunn had figured out that I was the Fordgythe Institute? Because he knew I had $100,000,000 in the bank?

"Because you did something funny with the Terwilliger Spoon."

I was so relieved that I practically laughed in his face. "Who are you?" I asked.

"Matt Jerkowicz."

Now I knew how I knew him. He was on the football team last year. I didn't care about football, but you don't forget a guy who's named "Jerkowicz." I had felt sorry for him from the moment I'd first heard his name. "Hi, Matt. I'm Jake."

"I know," he said.

"Oh, yeah, of course. So, this is about the Terwilliger Spoon?"

"Yeah. Old man Mr. Dunn thinks you had something to do with it going missing. He asked me to check up on you." He held his pencil on a blank sheet on his pad, ready to record whatever I said.

"We found the spoon. We were doing a favor for Amanda. And now her father treats me like a criminal? That's nice."

"They're all very confused about what went on with that spoon. It was gone. It was back. It was back again."

"Yeah, I can see that that's pretty confusing. But I've got nothing else to say. Besides, I have to go do my chores."

Matt closed his notebook. "Ok, well, thanks. I'll tell Mr. Dunn that."

"Are you done following me?"

"Yeah, I guess so. No offense." He started to turn away.

"Hey, Matt," I called. "Do you have a minute?"

It didn't take more than a sundae at The Soda Squirt to find out a few interesting facts from Matt. First, Mr. Dunn was constantly making phone calls to the editor of *The Register*. Every little detail had to be approved by Mr. Dunn. And then there were all the bad ideas he came up with that the editor would have to find a way to ignore. Matt's favorite was Mr. Dunn's brilliant idea that the paper ought to highlight in yellow the key phrases in each article so readers could skim. When the editor had argued that that they might as well just reduce each article to three or four sentences, Mr. Dunn had actually thought it was a good idea.

I also learned that Mr. Dunn was obsessed with the upcoming debate. He had most of the staff of *The Register* researching his side of the argument. In fact, Matt said that Mr. Dunn was even thinking that he might run for governor if this debate went well. He had hired a professional media coach, someone who teaches you how to be effective on television. Worst, Mr. Dunn had a full-size photograph of my father in his office, and of course it was a photo of him from the Pancake Breakfast with the syrup running into his collar. Mr. Dunn was practicing his debating techniques looking straight into the photograph's eyes. "I will destroy him," he said whenever anyone came into his office. "Destroy him!"

My father didn't have that kind of focus. Or obsession.

It was scary.

But not as scary as the thought that if I had had time recently to drop off stacks of cash from the Fordgythe Foundation, Matt would have found me out. But things had been pretty hectic what with school ending and the debate coming up, so it had been a week since my last donation.

But now that Matt wouldn't be following me, I could saddle up my bike.

There were eight high school seniors who I knew were going to have trouble affording college. They each got $10,000, neatly tied with my mother's pretty yarn.

The local hospital got $20,000 to refurnish the entire maternity ward. I'd read in *The Gaz* that they didn't even have enough beds for moms.

Mr. Grubach, who had been teaching art at our school for the past hundred years, was retiring. He was the only person who could tell what my drawings were supposed to look like. Everyone else would ask me if I was drawing a rumpled bed or a pile of leaves, but Mr. Grubach would come up to me and say: "Nice horse, Jake." The Fordgythe Foundation gave him $10,000 for a trip to Italy and France to see those artworks he was always telling us about.

I was careful making the deliveries. I was sure nobody with antennas coming out of his head was watching me.

My father was practicing again when I came back. He had piles of papers in front of him and was scribbling notes on yellow pads of paper. Unlike Mr. Dunn, he wasn't having his employees come up with good one-liners and clever ways of making my father look bad. But my father believed that the truth always wins. That's why he's a journalist.

I guess I don't believe that the truth always wins. Well-told lies win all too often. That's why we have commercials.

I wished there was something I could do for my father. He was more convinced than I was that the lottery was a bad idea. Just because the lottery made me rich didn't mean that the state ought to have a lottery in the first place. I was just lucky. Still, I didn't think a lottery was such a terrible thing. If I had to vote, I'd vote against having one because I think my father's reasoning is right. But I didn't think it was as big a deal as he did.

Nevertheless, I sure wanted my dad to win. In fact, I'll do what my father would do: List the reasons.

First, I thought he was right.

Second, I didn't like Mr. Dunn, even though he had been nice to Ari.

Third, I didn't want Mr. Dunn to be able to use winning the debate to help him become governor of the state.

Fourth, Dad's my father.

You could take away reasons 1-3 and #4 would have been enough.

But I couldn't figure out anything I could do to help him.

So, I asked my mother.

"That's very nice of you, Jake," she said, "But I think he has to do this on his own."

"I heard you helping him rehearse the other night."

"Yes, well, that didn't go too well. He's so nervous about this that he won't listen to criticism…I mean the sort of helpful criticism that would help him do better."

"Yeah, I could tell," I said. "Maybe he'd rehearse better with me."

"Well, you can try, but I wouldn't count on it."

Dad didn't go for it. He didn't want anyone helping him rehearse.

I did have one idea, though. It meant placing a call to Ms. Minden. Julia.

"Sounds great," Julia said. "I'll get to work on it right away."

That Friday, Ari and I made a trip into the city. Video games were turning out to be the one treat I could buy for myself without arousing anyone's suspicion, because I kept them at Ari's whose house was such a mess that his parents would never notice the sudden increase in the number of video games in his room. But we were afraid that the creepy guy who runs the Game Dungeon in town would start wondering how we could afford to buy every new game that came out. So, after school we hopped onto the train to find a game store in the city.

It was good to spend some time with Ari alone. I'd been hanging out more with Mimi for the past few weeks, not quite on purpose but not quite by accident either. Ari could be sort of annoying even if he was one of my two best friends.

But something amazing happened on the train ride back: Ari was normal.

The car was crowded with commuters leaving work a little early on Friday afternoon. We found two seats facing each other and were about to sit when Halley came down the aisle. I hadn't seen her since the day we spent at the old age center. Ari and I both like Halley a lot. She's always friendly and almost always cheerful. I said hello, but Ari stood up from his seat and offered it to her. He didn't even seem to have thought about it.

Now, this might sound like plain old sexism: the gallant young knight offering the damsel his seat. But it wasn't. Halley has a problem with her spine and has difficulty standing for more than a few minutes. That's why Amanda's handing her stuff for Halley to carry at the Senior Center was especially thoughtless. Anyway, by offering Halley his seat, Ari was simply doing the right thing.

He stood for the entire trip – I offered to swap positions with him halfway through, but he refused – having a conversation with Halley that wasn't awkward, self-centered or dumb.

Our little Ari was growing up.

When we got to his house with our bundle of video games, I asked him straight out: "Ari, how come you weren't a dork with Halley?"

"Why would I be a dork?"

"Because you always are. You get nervous, you say completely obvious things, you ride your bike into the bushes…"

"Ok ok," he said, embarrassed. "I used to do that. And it was a pretty good technique. It really worked."

"Worked?"

"I'm shy," he explained, popping a new game into the console. "Maybe you've noticed."

"Once or twice."

"I don't make friends easily. That's why you're like my only friend."

"There's Mimi…"

"She's more your friend than my friend."

"That's not true." I knew that it was.

"If you weren't my friend, she'd never have starting be friends with me."

"That's not true." I knew that it was.

"So, being a dork gave me a reason why I have trouble with people."

"Really? I thought being a dork was why you have trouble with people." I know it sounds like we were saying the same thing, but we understood that we weren't: Dorkiness was Ari's solution to his problem with people, not the cause of it.

"So, how did this come about?" I asked. "Did you just wake up one day and say: 'I am not a dork'?"

"Actually, it was sort of like that. Let me tell you…"

It seems that for the past 130 years, Ari had had a crush on Mimi. (That covers his entire life plus several past lives.) Even when he was chasing Amanda, his heart still belonged to Mimi. I was a dope not to see it.

So, last week, while walking home from school with Mimi, he wondered why he was able to talk comfortably with her whereas when he saw Amanda, he pretty much just leaped into whatever solid object was nearby. But that's not what he asked Mimi. Instead he said: "I haven't seen much of you and Jake recently."

"End of school. Busy. You know." Ari knew Mimi was lying. Mimi and I had definitely been avoiding him.

Ari decided that it was time to let Mimi know how he felt. So, he went home and did the most dorkish thing he could think of. Of course, he didn't think it was dorkish. It just naturally was. He baked her a giant cookie in the shape of a heart. And, being Ari, he decided that if one recipe was good, two recipes would be even better, so he picked the best ingredients from his mother's chocolate chip cookies and her peanut butter oatmeal cookies. And, what the heck, he dumped in the best ingredients in cheesecake because everyone likes cheesecake. Then he spelled out "Mimi Your Special" in licorice candies. (Too bad his cake didn't come with a spellchecker.)

He baked it. He cut off the burned parts. He ate most of the burned parts. He put it in a pizza box that had only a few large grease stains in it. He carried it to Mimi's house and left it on her stoop. Where the sprinkler soaked it. And squirrels ran across it. And Mimi slipped on it when she came out the door. Bam, off her stoop and down on the ground.

"That's from me," Ari said as he helped Mimi up. Her face went from scrunched-up annoyance to wide-open smile.

Mimi being Mimi said, "Oh, that's so nice of you, Ari" even before she opened the box.

The cookie inside had crumbled. The licorice pieces were now in a code that no human would ever decipher. "Well, it's the thought," she said as she carefully didn't eat any of the sopping wet, squished, squirrel-nibbled cookie. She smiled at him. "What *was* the thought, anyway?"

Ari knew he was not going to be able to get the words out. After all, that's why he baked the cookie. The cookie would do the speaking for him. Except the cookie not only had no words on it any more, it had attacked Mimi. Without his cookie to tell Mimi how he felt, he knew he would stand there, stammer something stupid, and then run away.

Instead, he said, "I've always liked you, Mimi."

"Me, too, Ari. That's nice of you to say."

"You know what I mean, though, don't you?"

Mimi looked at him. At first she smiled as if she were about to make a joke. Then she thought about what it meant to have him say such words to her. Her smile deepened. "Yes, Ari, I do. I've known for a long time."

"But you never said anything," Ari said.

"Neither did you."

"But do you like me? I mean the way I like you."

"I don't know," Mimi said. "It was easier avoiding that question when you were being the dopey guy you usually are. You know, the guy who leaves a pizza on my front step so that I slip on it and scrape my calf."

"It was actually a cookie that said 'You're Special.'"

"Aw, that's sweet. But it's a lot harder answering the question to the Ari who's speaking to me like a real human being about what he feels."

"That's ok. You don't have to answer," he said.

"I want to. I just don't know. I feel like I have to get to know this Ari." Mimi has a wonderful smile, you know.

As they went through the gate to the sidewalk, Mimi asked Ari the obvious question: "What happened to you?"

"You smiled at me."

"That's awfully romantic, but..."

"No," he said, "I don't mean that you smiled and suddenly the roses bloomed and the rain stopped. I mean I tripped you on your steps, but as soon as you realized that it was me, you smiled. And, I don't know, I felt like I had always been two people but hadn't known it. One person is the awkward, geeky Ari who can never say the right thing, the one who would bake you a cookie because he knows he won't be able to say what he wants to say. The other person is the person you've known all your life. And that's the one you smiled at."

"That's really cool."

"Yeah. The thing is, though, that I think I'm probably still a dork."

"Probably," Mimi said as she kissed him on the cheek in a way that Ari spent the next three days trying to figure out.

Ari was just finishing telling me this when I heard my father come in. Since I didn't know what to say either – Mimi and Ari seemed like a pretty unlikely match, even if this was a New and Not-So-Dorky Ari – I went downstairs and greeted him. He was carrying a copy of the latest *The Gaz.* I took it upstairs where Ari and I found three interesting things about it.

First, just about all the local advertisers had a coupon promising that for everything you bought there, the Fordgythe Foundation would donate 10% to a local charity, up to a total of a million dollars. You didn't get a discount, but you knew that you were helping someone else. I thought lots of people would prefer that to *the Register's* offer. Julia had done a great job getting the advertisers to agree.

Second, the lead story on the front page was headlined "Who Is Fordgythe?" The story listed about half of the donations we had made. Although it didn't get very far in pinpointing who was behind the foundation, it did point out that the foundation wasn't legally registered in the state, or in any other state for that matter. No street address, no names listed, no web page. It made the Fordgythe Foundation sound fishy, although the article pointed out that all the donations it could find were to good causes.

Third, my father's editorial this week was about why we should be careful about accepting money from a foundation about which we know nothing. It could be embarrassing. In fact, the editorial said that *The Gaz* would no longer accept ads that feature coupons from the Fordgythe Foundation. My father apologized for letting them go into this issue. "Our guess is that there is a single person behind this Foundation," the editorial said. "Its pattern of donations and its way of behaving are too quirky for a Foundation run by a committee. If so, and if the Fordgythe Foundation really has the best interests of our town at heart," the editorial concluded, "let it uncloak itself to remove the suspicion that its secrecy is motivated by shame and its donations are motivated by guilt."

Ulp. Dad was coming after me pretty hard. And he didn't even know it.

Chapter 22

While *The Gaz* carefully laid out what was known about the Fordgythe Foundation, *The Register* spouted rumors and assumptions as if it were a whale with a size XL blow hole. If you were to believe the article on its front page, the Fordgythe Foundation was a plot by outsiders to undermine the moral fabric of our town, its money very likely came from drug lords trying to "launder" their cash so the tax people couldn't trace it, and it was out personally to sink *The Register* by pretending to give money to charities for purchases made at local stores.

Most interesting of all to me were *The Register's* clear hints that it was on the verge of exposing who was behind the Foundation. Since I knew that I wasn't a drug lord laundering cash, I also knew that *The Register* wasn't truly close to figuring it out. The one thing they'd gotten right, though, was that the Foundation was trying to sink *The Register*, if by "sink" you mean "keep *The Register* from sinking *The Gaz*."

Here's the thing my father figured out that *The Register* didn't. My father understood, based on nothing but intuition, that the Fordgythe Foundation was personal. It may have the word "foundation" in its title, but it's really about one person – and his two friends – helping out other individuals. *The Register* assumed it was a heartless organization giving cash to other nameless individuals. People so often see their own reflections when they look at others. That's why *The Register* missed the point.

There was only a week until the debate, and I knew my

family life was going to be busy and tense. But I decided it'd be worth it to try to throw *The Register* off. I didn't want *The Gaz* to find out who was behind The Foundation, but I definitely wanted *The Register* to be very wrong in public about it.

Meanwhile, another of my plans was about to kick in. This one was only a little bit sneaky, though. I had asked Julia, my employee, to find someone who could help my father do better in the debate. She had done some research and found a "media consultant" named Mischa Buskin, who claimed to have worked with the biggest stars, politicians and heads of companies, teaching them how to come across well on TV. Julia sent me the Web address for Mischa's company, which was called TeleSuccess, Inc. The site said that the company would teach you how to hold your hands while on camera, how often to smile, and "The Seven Gestures of Success." Sounded pretty dumb to me, but if you've ever seen someone interviewed on TV who didn't know where to look or how to hold his hands, you realize that there are some simple, dumb things that make a big difference.

So, my father got a fat, glossy package from TeleSuccess, Inc. sent to him by The Fordgythe Foundation. Because of the Foundation's interest in eliminating state lotteries, the letter said, it was paying for a three hour session with Mischa Buskin. Further, because the Foundation understood how busy my father is and how soon the debate is to be held, rather than requiring my father to fly out to Los Angeles, they were flying Mr. Buskin in. He could be there any day of the week. The letter ended by saying that a representative of the Foundation would call immediately to set up the visit.

Because the envelope was from the Foundation, it was the first one in the daily pile my father opened when he came home on Monday night. He read it once, shook his head in disbelief, and then read it again. "I'll be," he said, not telling us what he would be. "I'll be. What sort of Foundation is this?"

"What is it, Dad?"

"The Fordgythe Foundation is trying to bribe me."

"What?" I said in genuine surprise.

"They're trying to bribe me," he explained completely unhelpfully, waving the paper in my face. "They're offering to fly some bogus media consultant out here to teach me how to fake being sincere."

"Really?" I said.

"Take a look," he said, handing me the packet. I read again the letter that Ms. Minden had written; I'd read it two nights before. "It doesn't sound like a bribe to me," I said.

"A bribe doesn't have to be money. If you get out of a speeding ticket by offering to wash the cop's car, that's still a bribe."

"Would that work?"

"Of course not! But that's not the point."

"I know," I said. "But I don't read this as a bribe at all. They're not trying to get you to change your opinion about lotteries. They're trying to help you do better."

"Yes, but…"

I interrupted my own father. "If they said we'll give you

media training or wash your car or leave $5,000 in your mailbox if you come out *against* the lottery, or if you'd do badly in the debate on purpose...*that'd* be a bribe."

"May I get a word in edgewise?" my father asked. "I agree that it's not your standard sort of bribe. Nevertheless, as I'm exposing the Fordgythe Foundation in the paper, if it were to get out that I'd accepted money expensive media training from them, it'd look very very bad. Journalists can't do that sort of thing."

"But, Dad..."

"It's a matter of Journalistic Ethics."

You could practically hear him capitalize the phrase "Journalistic Ethics." Those capitals meant the conversation was over. But this time I wasn't giving up. "But, Dad, you know how you just said, 'May I get a word in edgewise?' when I had only talked for about a minute? That's exactly the type of little thing that puts people off. It's what you need media training for."

"Gee," said my father, "you seem to know an awful lot about media training all of a sudden."

"He's right," my mother said, entering the room. She'd been listening from the den. "I'm sure there are a hundred little ways anyone's presentation skills could be improved. Something like 'May I get a word in edgewise?' is the type of little thing that can prevent an audience from hearing what you're actually saying. And that's the point."

"I'm going to be myself on TV..." my father insisted.

"No one is saying you shouldn't be," my mother said, sweetly. "That's what we all want. But how much of an expert are you on how to present ideas on TV? A big expert or just a pretty big expert?"

"I'm not an..."

"No, you're not an expert at all. But I promise you that Mr. Dunn has been through the training. He's an expert. And that means it's going to be easier for the audience to agree with him than it will be to agree with you. I think you ought to take the Foundation up on the offer."

"Out of the question. I simply cannot accept gifts of any kind from an organization I'm investigating. And I will not become something I'm not on TV just because some media expert thinks he knows what type of phoniness looks really sincere. That's all there is to it."

And that was all there was to it. I emailed Ms. Minden and told her to tell Mischa not to bother packing his bags. He charged us "only" $2,000 for reserving the time to see my father.

After dinner, I had an idea about how to throw *The Register* off the scent. I called Ms. Minden again and asked if she could meet me at the Soda Squirt.

"Sure, boss," she replied. Wow. I was a boss.

She was there right on time. "What's up, boss?" she asked.

"Could you stop calling me 'boss'?"

"Sure thing ... boss. Ok, I'll stop."

"Thanks."

"But you are my boss, you know."

"Ok, ok, and you're my slave. But can we just keep it down?" There was no one else in the restaurant.

"Ok. How can I help you, oh my little captain?"

"Suppose the money for the Foundation were coming from Germany," I said. "Would there be any receipts or forms or anything that would show that?"

"Yes, sure. Depending on how the money was transferred from Germany to here, there might be a few different types of forms that get filed. Why do you ask? Are you thinking of moving your money to Germany?"

"No, I'm thinking about ways to give *The Register* the entirely wrong idea about who's behind the Fordgythe Foundation."

"Aha!" Ms. Minden said happily. "You want to get one of those forms, don't you?"

"Yes. But not an entire form. I just want to include a scrap, as if by accident."

"But not enough for him to be able to trace it back to a particular bank in Germany because he'd find out that there is no bank account there for the Fordgythe Foundation."

"That's what I was thinking," I said.

"And it's a darn good thought. That shouldn't be a problem. I can photocopy a real one from a different account and tear it so that he can see that it came from Germany but not see which bank or which account."

"That sounds perfect," I said.

"And best of all, it's not even illegal! I like working for you, but I'm not willing to go to jail for you."

"'No lies, no actual crimes.' That should be the motto of the Fordgythe Foundation."

"I can do this tomorrow. It'll be fun!" Ms. Minden slid out of the booth and out the door, smiling.

I paid for her coffee. I was, after all, her boss.

Chapter 23

It was the Friday before the debate on Sunday and my family was a mess.

My father was, of course, more stressed than I'd ever seen. He wanted to do well in this debate because he cared about the issue. And this debate was his big audition. If he did well, he might get to do this regularly. I could see why that would be fun, but I had had no idea that my father thought it would be fun, too.

Stress is a communicable disease like measles. You can catch it from others, particularly from people you're close to. My father was not being particularly nice that week. He snapped at my mother when she didn't deserve it. Well, not that she ever deserves it. He wasn't doing his chores because he was so focused on preparing. He was just a big bundle of nerves and no fun to live with.

But that was just the beginning for my mother. She was preparing to teach a couple of courses and was supposed to be sending in the list of books her students would be buying in the fall. That meant designing the courses, both of which were new ones for her. So, with a deadline coming up, she was reading through big stacks of books, trying to figure out what she'd be teaching week by week.

As if that weren't enough, Maddie picked this week to come home from pre-school with head lice. Same as last year. At first you think having lice is disgusting, and you're right. Then you think it's embarrassing, which it also is. But if you've been through having lice once before, mainly you think it is just a major pain in the butt. My mother had to run everything through the washer and dryer. And then we all had to undergo The Treatment. (There's a reason why the world's great supermodels don't wash their hair with lice shampoo.) And then, twice a day, my mother had to pick through Maddie's long hair, looking for the tiny eggs lice leave attached to strands of hair. And, Maddie had a cold so it was hard to get her to sit still long enough to do a thorough job of it. Maddie would squirm, my mother would get annoyed, Maddie would cry, my mother would try not to yell…

I, of course, was a rock. I was calm, always cheerful, helpful and just a delight to be around.

Yeah, sure. I was worried that one of the newspapers would figure out who was behind the Foundation. I was worried what that would do to my father in the debate. I was worried Mr. Dunn would be better trained than my dad. I was worried that if I were found out, I had dug such a deep hole for myself that my parents would never speak to me again. I hadn't lied to them, not even once, but I sure had gone out of my way to keep my $100,000,000 secret from them. At some point, keeping a secret begins to feel a lot like lying.

So, when my father came on Friday with copies of *The Gaz* and *The Register*, it took all of my self-control not to rip the copies out of his hands. I made myself walk upstairs one step at a time to read them.

The Gaz had an article about the Fordgythe Foundation on page five, right next to an article about how the high school's football field was being re-seeded. It reported on some of our recent donations but had no more news about who was behind the Foundation. "Our investigation is continuing," was all it said.

The Register had us all over the front page. There was a photo of Arnie Junger holding the bills I'd given him for his college education. "Local youth says he was surprised by the $10,000 he found in his mailbox." Well, wouldn't you be?

The headline of the lead article screamed: "The Fordgythe-Germany Connection! *The Register* Cracks the Case!" It began:

> As the result of an extensive investigation by *The Register*'s award-winning investigative journalism team, we have learned that the "Fordgythe Foundation" is in fact a front for German financial interests.

> The break in the case came as a result of sloppiness on the part of "The Foundation," probably because they have been made nervous by *The Register*'s intense investigative journalism efforts.

> "The Foundation" left a scrap of a funds transfer form in a "donation" it left for local high school senior, Arnold Junger. *The Register* has confirmed that the fund transfer came from a German-based bank. We continue our efforts to discover exactly which bank it was.

Of course, they don't mention that their "investigative journalism" consisted of opening the package I'd sent to Arnold.

I'd chosen his package as the one to "accidentally" contain the funds transfer form because I knew that Arnold was Mr. Dunn's nephew. And he was interning at *the Register*, so I sent it to him at work. I was pretty sure that even *The Register*'s crack investigative journalism team wouldn't miss that clue.

The Register had not only fallen for it, they had wrapped it in some very bad writing.

At dinner I asked my father about it. "It looks like *The Register* has cracked the Fordgythe Foundation case," I said.

"I doubt it," he replied, stabbing at his peas with an unusual fierceness.

"Why is it that?" my mother asked.

"He's got one scrap of a funds transfer form. There are a thousand reasons why that could have been included in with a cash donation. And one of those reasons could even be that the Fordgythe people are trying to throw *The Register* off the scent."

"That'd be devious," my mother said. She smiled at my father. He smiled back as much as he could given that he wasn't smiling much these days.

That smile made me more nervous than anything I'd read in either newspaper.

Sunday was the big day, so on Saturday if our house had been tense before, now it was like one of those balsa wood airplanes with a rubber band turned so many times that the knots have knots on top of their knots.

Mimi and Ari came over to take me out. "Let's go spend

some of that German money," Mimi said.

"Did you leave that German form in the packet on purpose?" Ari asked.

"Accidents happen," I said, smiling.

It was a beautiful night. As we got on the train to the city the sky was the color of the summer ocean. I checked to make sure that my backpack was tightly zipped and that the straps were in good shape.

"You want to go to a fancy restaurant?" Mimi asked excitedly.

"Actually, not really," I said.

"Good," Mimi said. "I was only pretending to want to in case you did."

"How about a Chinese restaurant?" Ari asked.

"Great idea," I replied. "Maybe we can find one that isn't mainly a take-out place. You know, one with table cloths and everything."

"Sure," Ari said. "So long as they have sweet and sour. The expensive ones don't have that."

"And fortune cookies," Mimi said.

So, that was our task: find the best Chinese restaurant that still had sweet and sour and fortune cookies. I like a challenge. But first, I had an errand.

The spot next to Salzburg Grille where Philip and Caroline had settled was no longer empty. New people had taken it over, two guys – probably in their twenties, although it can be hard to tell – sleeping on a blanket. I didn't want to wake them, so we went next door and ordered four complete steak dinners to go. They were still asleep when we came back, so we left the bag between them. I put $1,000 at the bottom of the bag along with a note from the Fordgythe Foundation.

"I hope they wake before the food gets cold," Mimi said.

"Maybe we should go back and wake them," Ari said.

"No, let's let them sleep," she said.

Now we just wandered looking for our perfect Chinese restaurant. Along the way we bought a very bad giant pretzel from a push cart vendor who looked to be my grandfather's age. While he hand the pretzel to Mimi, I slipped a thousand dollar bill into the coffee can where he kept his money.

We passed by a literacy clinic that teaches adults how to read. I went into a fast food joint's rest room and tied up $30,000 with some of my mother's yarn and packed the bundle and a Fordgythe note into one of the envelopes I'd brought with me. I shoved it through the clinic's mail slot. "Remind me to have Ms. Minden call first thing on Monday to make sure that they got it," I said.

We passed by a co-op store, the sort of place that sells whole-grain foods and lets people who can't afford to pay work there a few hours a week instead. It had signs up trying to raise money to clean up the river. When the clerk was busy elsewhere, I stuffed ten $1,000 bills into the coffee can where you make donations.

A cab driver told us that he sends money back to his family in Haiti every week. He said he was saving money to bring them to the United States. When we got out of the cab, I gave him an envelope with $15,000 in it, but nothing identifying it as coming from The Foundation. "This is an extra tip. Don't open it until after your next rider leaves," I said. "And don't tell anyone that you got it from kids."

Our next stop took us past the Grille. The two men were awake now. The remains of their dinner were scattered around them.

"Hello," I said. "Good dinner."

At first neither spoke. They looked at each other. The taller one said, "Yeah. Really good," eyeing us suspiciously.

"Why don't you get out of here. Quit staring."

Ari stepped in. "We're not staring. We're the ones..." I tugged on Ari's sleeve to get him to stop.

"Who did what? Get out of here before I call a cop."

"We didn't do anything wrong..."

"You're bothering me," the man said. "This is our space. Go on back to your rich kid home."

"Come on," I said, "let's leave them be."

"Bye" Mimi said. "Good luck."

We left, confused by what had happened.

"I feel terrible," Mimi said.

"Me, too," I said. "They weren't very nice."

"They were nervous about having so much money on them," Ari said.

We passed a veterans' center. They got an instant grant of $25,000 from the Fordgythe Foundation. It was more than I would have given normally, but I was making up for the rejection we'd just been handed.

"I'm getting really hungry," Ari said.

"This place looks promising," Mimi said, reading the menu of a Chinese restaurant a few doors down from the veteran's center. It seemed to have it all, right down to the fortune cookies. It was a little expensive, but what the heck.

I looked in my backpack. I patted my pockets. "You know what?" I asked. "I gave away all my money."

Ari and Mimi looked at each other. Between us we had $21 and three train tickets back. "So we'll find a cheaper place to eat," Mimi said.

Eighteen dollars later, we were full and ready to go home.

Chapter 24

The debate was at seven at night. By four o'clock, we were all dressed, my father had shined his shoes, and my mother had checked Maddie one more time for lice. We were a family clean and ready for TV.

The station was in the city, so we took the train in. The conductor recognized me, impressing my parents. "You're becoming quite the traveler," my mother said. I only hoped that we didn't end up in a cab with one particular Haitian driver.

Fortunately, the TV station was just a few blocks from the train station. It's odd that both TVs and trains have stations since they're really not very much alike. While the train station was made of grimy brick and concrete, the TV station was all glass, colorful walls and carpet. The producer of the show, a woman about my mother's age named Laurie Brooks, showed my family to the "green room" where the guests wait before they go on air.

Needless to say, the green room wasn't green. It was a light tan. There were some not-very-comfortable couches, more mirrors than I like to see, a television set tuned to that station's broadcast, and a table with fruit, stale donuts and coffee. Maddie went straight for one of the donuts. She doesn't care if the donut is fresh or stale so long as it's topped with icing.

My father sat down and immediately opened up his bulging notebook of ideas, notes and clippings.

"Don't you think you ought to take a break?" my mother asked. "You're going to over-prepare."

"I don't even know what that means," my father replied, not looking up. "How can you be too prepared?"

"You can be too rehearsed. You know what you believe, you know all the facts that exist, you have your arguments all set..."

"Good idea. Jake, will you test me on these facts?" he asked, handing me what must have been fifteen pages stapled together.

"Don't, Jake," my mother said.

"Torn between two parents!" I replied. "Don't you know what this does to my delicate emotional state?"

"We'll pay for your psychiatrist," my father said, the closest he'd come to a joke in a week. I was going to be very glad when this debate was over.

My father took the packet of facts back from me and started studying on his own. My mother stood up. "Maybe we should leave your father alone to over-prepare himself."

Just as she started to lead Maddie away from the snack table, the door opened and in came Mr. Dunn with Amanda and three men in suits. He stood in the doorway for a moment, looking disapprovingly at the sofa, the food, and finally my father.

My father stood up but Mr. Dunn made no move to come greet him. "Hello," my father said. "Ready for a good, honest debate?"

Amanda pinched a donut and dropped it in disgust.

"I'm ready to take on those who would deny our citizens the

right to choose their own form of amusement," answered Mr. Dunn. One of the men in suits leaned into him and whispered in his ear. "Who don't trust our citizens to choose their own form of amusement," Mr. Dunn corrected himself. Apparently "trust" was a key word for him to work into the debate.

"Well," my father said, perhaps regretting not taking up the Fordgythe Foundation's offer to fly Mischa out, "I'm sure it will be a good, spirited debate. That's what democracy is all about."

"Democracy is all about trusting citizens to choose their own form of entertainment," said Mr. Dunn, looking at the man in the suit for approval. The man nodded.

My mother said, "Honey, I'm taking the kids out for a bite to eat. Would you like to join us?"

"No, I need to…"

"Please do join us," my mother said firmly.

Once the door to the green room closed my mother said, "I wasn't going to leave you there for another minute with that awful man. Let's go get a cup of coffee and a real donut. That'll be much better for you than sitting there as Mr. Dunn uses you for target practice."

"He's good," my father said.

"He's over-prepared," my mother replied.

Apparently we took too long because when we came back, Laurie the producer was very glad to see us. "Thank goodness! We have to get you right into makeup." My father made a face, which Laurie immediately understood. "If we don't put on makeup," she explained, "you won't look the way you actually do."

She led us to the chair where the makeup person started dusting him with powder. I made sure not to make fun of my father, tempting though it was. Laurie patted my father on the shoulder, and said "You'll do fine. That other man's just a bully." Then she led us to our seats.

The studio was quite small with room for about 50 people, although, as a camera showed us, it looked much bigger when broadcast. I think that's because if you show a row of ten people on TV, the viewer assumes that the row extends in both directions even when it doesn't, like being on the ocean and assuming that the sea keeps going over past the horizon. Except you're right when it comes to the ocean.

We were almost the first people there. Laurie pointed to a woman standing in the back of the theatre. "That's Margaret Houle. She's in charge of all programming for the station. If she likes how your father does today…" She left the sentence hanging and then said, "Well, I have to be getting back. I'm sure your father will do well. People will just like him when they hear him. I have an eye for these things." I was sure she was right. Of course, my father didn't want to be liked. He wanted to convince people that the lottery is a bad idea.

The studio was beginning to fill up. I recognized a few people who worked for Mr. Dunn, and most of the tiny staff of *The Gaz* was there as well. Otherwise, there was only one face that I recognized: Mrs. Fordgythe. She was in the back on the other side. She waved to me. I gave a quick wave back.

"Who's that, dear?" my mother asked.

"Someone I met on line at the Herb's Pick-a-Chick store."

"She must be nice to remember you."

"Yeah, she seemed very nice."

Ms. Houle was still standing in the back, her arms crossed. Waiting.

The moderator of the event was the local television anchorperson, Lola Freitag. On TV she seemed to be the sort of person who could only speak from cue cards, although when she talked to the audience five minutes before the show started, she was actually quite good. She explained the rules of the half-hour debate and sternly told us not to applaud except when the "Applause" light went on. "You'll just be taking time away from the person you're applauding for," she said.

A sign that tells you when to applaud. That really seems wrong.

My father and Mr. Dunn came out from the same side of the studio and walked to their podiums. From the way they didn't look at each other, it seemed that they hadn't gotten any friendlier. Mr. Dunn stood there, as straight as a column holding up a porch. He stared directly in front of him, his hands held just above the waist, bent at the elbows, undoubtedly as he had been taught at media school. My father was bowed over his podium, frantically spreading out notes, running his hands through his hair exactly as media school would have told him not to.

"Welcome to the great debate on the state lottery," said Lola

Freitag, and so it began. As Lola introduced the two debaters, the camera focused on each. There were monitors in the studio, of course, so we could see what the home viewers could see. Mr. Dunn looked like he was a senior news anchor, completely at home in front of the camera. My father looked like he had slept in his clothes and was slightly confused about why he was there.

Lola explained the rules. Each debater was going to be given three minutes to present his point of view. Then Lola would ask each of them some questions "to clarify their points of view." Then the two debaters would get to ask each other questions. Finally, they'd each get a minute to conclude. It sounded simple, yet I was scared purple, especially about the part when Mr. Dunn would get to ask my father questions. I was sure that his team had worked long and hard on coming up with the questions that would make my father look as bad as possible. My father meanwhile had focused on questions that he thought would bring a reasonable person closer to the truth. The problem was that Mr. Dunn didn't intend to be reasonable. He intended to win.

Despite starting off looking fidgety, I thought my father did great in his opening statement. True, even though he had timed himself over and over to make sure that he came in under three minutes, he ended up having to rush through the last fifteen seconds, covering the last two points in just a couple of sentences and without inhaling. That aside, he did great.

Mr. Dunn did better. Even though I disagreed with him and could see the holes in what he was saying, I had to admit that unless your father had been lecturing you all your life about why the lottery is a bad idea, you would have found Mr. Dunn's opening comments persuasive. Plus, it was as if he was relaxing at his kitchen table after dinner, slowly and calmly explaining himself, confident that he was right and enjoying himself. He was good at TV.

My hopes that Lola would ask the questions that would show everyone what was wrong with Mr. Dunn's argument were dashed as soon as she opened her mouth. I could see that she was reading the questions off a printed sheet. They had nothing to do with what either my father or Mr. Dunn had just said. If anything, they were harder on my father than on Mr. Dunn. For example, she asked my father what taxes he would raise to make up for the money the state would lose if it cancelled the lottery. Dad answered well, I thought: "We might not have to raise taxes. We might move the money from other programs. But, Ms. Freitag, the point to remember is that the lottery is itself a tax, a tax on the poorest in our state. We target advertisements at them, convincing them that they can magically escape their poverty, and the money that we gather from them is taken out of their community and used to finance the educational system for the rich as well as the poor. Our poorest communities are losers in this system."

Lola might have followed up on this. She might have asked if my father would be satisfied if the state government stopped advertising the lottery. She might have asked if he'd be satisfied if more of the money that was raised was given to poor neighborhoods instead of spreading it evenly across all communities. But those questions weren't on her prepared sheet, so she instead asked Mr. Dunn what I thought was a

254

much easier question: "Are there any changes you'd make to the lottery system at all?" Mr. Dunn said that he'd run it more often and offer more and bigger prizes. Nice. You can't go wrong offering people more money more often.

I only half-listened to these questions and answers. The other half of me was trying to figure out what Mr. Dunn was going to ask my father. And the remaining part me – which, when you add two halves together doesn't leave much left over – was listening to Maddie complaining to my mother that she had to go to the bathroom. "Can you hold it for another few minutes?" my mother asked.

"I really have to go."

My mother sighed and started to get up. Just then Mr. Dunn got to ask his first question of my father. "Mr. Richter, I understand that you are personally quite strongly opposed to the lottery. But is your family equally opposed?"

"I don't see what that has to do with anything," my father replied.

"You will once I tell you who is truly behind the Fordgythe Foundation." My mother sat down again and when Maddie started to whine, she cut her off. "You'll just have to hold it in for a few more minutes." Maddie frowned but stopped whining.

"I thought you already cracked that one, Mr. Dunn. The Germans."

Mr. Dunn's faced turned an ugly violet color. I thought he might be having trouble breathing but then I realized that it was how he blushed. He did it so infrequently that it made his face look like it was bruised. "That was based on preliminary information…"

"Plastered all over your front page on Friday," my father said. He didn't seem fidgety and awkward any more. "So, you realize that your big breakthrough article is all wrong?"

"It was based on preliminary information. But our further investigation has turned up something even more interesting. Let me ask you: Do you think the Fordgythe Foundation is doing remarkably good work?" Mr. Dunn sure had changed his tone about the Foundation. Except now I felt like I had to go to the bathroom. I didn't like where this was heading.

"Overall, I'd have to say, yes, the Fordgythe Foundation has been a blessing to this town," my father said, to my great relief. "Some of the donations seem a little eccentric, but it's brought relief to people who need it and it's supported organizations that help the neediest in our town. But from the editorials you've been writing about it, you, Mr. Dunn, seem to think it's something like a gangster organization. I believe your newspaper reported that it's being funded by drug money."

"Preliminary investigation," Mr. Dunn muttered quickly. "I am glad that you and I are in agreement on this crucial point. The Fordgythe Foundation has been a positive force in our community." He paused for a drink of water that he probably didn't need. It increased the suspense, though.

"I don't see what this has to do with the lottery," my father said.

Lola took this opportunity to say, "You're supposed to be asking a question, Mr. Dunn…" but my father looked at her, patted the air in front of him, and nodded to say that he was ok with the way it was going.

Mr. Dun carefully put down the glass of water and adjusted his tie. "Suppose I were to tell you that we have discovered that the Fordgythe Foundation is in fact funded entirely and completely by the mystery winner of the $111,000,000 lottery jackpot awarded a few months ago."

The audience didn't breath. The silence was noticeable. I could feel all the blood leaving my face. I'm not sure where it went, but I was positive my face was white with fear about what was about to happen. My mother looked at me, concerned.

Mr. Dunn's gaze swept the audience from one side to another as his tight-lipped smile seemed to say, "You agree that I just won the debate, don't you?"

As Mr. Dunn was about to talk again, my father said, "I know. The winner is my son."

The audience gasped. The camera looked at my father. It looked at Mr. Dunn. It looked at Lola. It looked back at my father who was staring straight at me. The camera followed his eyes and found me. It zoomed in until all you could see was my face, white as snow, and next to me Maddie jumping up and down in her seat, yelling, "Yay! We won! I get 10 dollars!" The things that little kids remember.

"Yes," thundered Mr. Dunn. "Your son! Your very own son! Ladies and gentlemen, here we have the living proof that good things come from the lottery. And not in some roundabout or complicated way, but right in the home of the leading opponent of the lottery. I rest my case." And with that, Mr. Dunn crossed his arms and leaned back, away from the microphone on his podium.

But my father didn't look like a man who had lost a debate. He stood up straighter. Suddenly his clothes hung on him right. His voice was firm. Looking directly at Mr. Dunn who refused to turn towards him, my father said, "How dare you, Mr. Dunn? How dare you? My son was given a lottery ticket by a kind elderly lady whom he had helped. He kept the fact that he won secret from everyone except a couple of friends because he knew we disapproved." How did my father know all this? "I only found out about this yesterday. My wife found out a few days before. We haven't even told our son that we know because we respect him. And let me tell you something: He has earned our respect. Can you imagine being a young man with such a secret? Can you imagine the sort of character it takes to do what he's done with the Fordgythe Foundation?"

My father looked at me. I think everyone in the audience, in the studio or at home, must have seen how much he loves me. It was embarrassing, but I'll never forget that look.

"So, you think you've made a mighty point about the lottery by betraying this good-hearted boy's secret. But you haven't at all. You think that you've proved that people who win the lottery use the money for good, giving back to the community. But you know that that's not true. People use the money for whatever they want to use the money for. Sometimes it's a tremendous help to them and their loved ones. And sometimes it destroys their lives. But that has nothing to do with why I'm opposed to the lottery. It's not because of what it does to the winners. It's because of what it does to the losers and what promoting the lottery does to our idea of what our government is about. I think that it turns our government into a casino that's trying to trick us out of our hard-earned money. But I've made that case here tonight and you've chosen to ignore it. Instead, you'd rather betray the secrets of the biggest-hearted child you'll ever have the privilege to meet."

But he wasn't done. "Let me be clear here tonight, Mr. Dunn. You see my son as a point you can use for your side. That's all he is to you. But the point doesn't even work. The fact is that what my son has done is truly exceptional. Who among us, if we'd won all that money, would think only about how best he could give it away? Who would find in his riches a connection to the poorest, the weakest, those most needing help? Would you, Mr. Dunn? Have you, Mr. Dunn? With all your riches, have you? You don't need to answer that. The fact is that my son is one in a one hundred and eleven million. So you can't use him as an argument in favor of the lottery. He's exceptional. That means he's what usually *doesn't* happen when people win a lottery."

Dad continued, "He's my son, Mr. Dunn, and you and this community are lucky that he's the one who won. And we are the luckiest parents in the world, not because our son won the lottery but because we have such a son. So, no, Mr. Dunn, your amazing fact doesn't change my mind one bit."

I think there was applause. Probably a lot. I know there was a whole bunch of hugging. I remember hugging Mrs. Fordgythe, and only reaching about a third of the way around her. And since the biggest hug came from my father and since I didn't go up on stage, I think the debate must have ended at that point.

One thing I remember very clearly, though: Maddie saying, "Oops. Too late."

Chapter 25

"How did you know?" What else was I going to ask? How's the weather? Do you know the first Pacific island that Magellan stopped at during his brave circumnavigation of the globe?

My parents had hurried me and Mrs. Fordgythe out of the studio before the press could catch us. We jumped into a taxi and were going to go to the train station, when my mother said, "The press will be waiting for us there." My parents looked at each other, shrugged their shoulders, and told the taxi driver to take us all the way home. Why not?

My mother said, "I was pretty sure last week because of the sorts of people who were getting donations. It seemed that a lot of places that our family cares about were getting money from the Fordgythe Foundation." For some reason, I was reminded of Mr. Sadler's cowboy story: "Know the people..." Of course, sometimes people you don't know need money, too.

"Of course," my mother said, "that was just a hunch. I didn't think it could really be true because, well, it was all so much. You set up a foundation. You were running an entire charity."

"So, how'd you figure it out?"

"An article in the paper said that the bundles of money were all tied with pink and purple yarn with little sparkly flecks in it. You think I wouldn't recognize my own yarn, Jake?"

"D'oh!" I said.

"So then I asked Ari."

"Figures!"

"But he wouldn't tell me a thing. So I asked Mimi."

"Mimi gave me away?"

"Well, yes. But only after I told her that I'd do my best to keep it a secret, and after I'd told her how proud I am of you."

"So, when did you tell Dad?"

"Yesterday. I had to. I knew Mr. Dunn was up to something. That awful Matt boy was snooping around. I think he was following you."

"I caught him at it last week but it was just about a missing spoon at the Dunns' house." My parents looked puzzled. "It's a long story."

"Well," said my mother, "I think Matt may not have told you the entire truth. I saw him following you on Saturday afternoon."

"He must have seen us in the city. We gave away a whole bunch of money on Saturday night."

"And here we thought you were wasting quarters in the arcade," my father said.

"Oh, we did that, too."

We dropped Mrs. Fordgythe off at her house. It was more like a mansion. The driveway went on long enough to need traffic signals. I got out of the taxi with her.

"I am so proud of you, my boy," she said, her hat blocking out all of the moon and half of the stars. She held my hand in

262

one of hers and patted it with her other.

"You're like my fairy godmother," I said to her.

"There's no such thing." She looked me straight in the eye and no longer seemed to be so flighty. "But if there were, I wouldn't have been *your* fairy godmother. Wouldn't I really have been the fairy godmother of all the people you've helped and all the people you're going to help?"

That's when I cried. She gave me another mountainous hug. "I so look forward to watching you grow," she said. "I so look forward to it."

• • •

So, here's the rest of what happened.

I was interviewed by every newspaper and television show on the planet and possibly some from other planets; that would explain some of the weird questions they asked me.

My mother became head of the Fordgythe Foundation. Ms. Minden was the second person in charge. That's a full-time job, so she quit her job at the bank.

My father still edits *The Gaz* because that's what he loves to do. He also enjoys the weekly news talk show he has on the TV station. Laurie is his producer.

The Gaz is now the number one newspaper in the region. *The Register* is still around but it just doesn't have the old oomph. Mr. Dunn doesn't have much to do with the paper any more. He keeps busy with the thousand other businesses he owns. But he's sure as heck not running for governor any time soon.

Soon after my mother became the head of the Foundation, we had a big family meeting, with Mrs. Fordgythe and Ari and Mimi. We also had a woman who knows all about managing money there; she was recommended by Ms. Harrigan at the bank. We got together to talk about how we want the Foundation to spend its money. The basic principle we came up with is simple: We should spend it where it will do the most good. Simple to say but really hard to put into practice. We decided that we wanted to continue to spend some in our town because those people are the closest to us – and not just in terms of distance – but that we also should look into donating money elsewhere in the world.

That conversation has turned into what seems like it will be, literally, a lifetime of conversations about how we can best spend the money that I won by accident, did nothing to earn, and don't deserve. I don't think there's any topic more interesting. But it's also hard because it means learning about the suffering so much of the world undergoes every day. Worse, it means choosing not to help some people who deserve it because, while $100,000,000 is a lot of money, it's nothing compared with the amount of money the world needs.

We decided that since much of the worst suffering is outside of this country, we ought to be helping out there, too. So, we've been all over the world. And my family has discovered that we love traveling. Often our journeys take us to places that make you sad and sometimes make you ashamed to be members of a species that lets such suffering happen, but we also go on trips for fun. We live at home as we always have, but we travel like rich people.

Of course, now that I don't have to hide my money from my parents, I also can spend it on myself more. But I don't enjoy spending money. I know it sounds odd, but when you realize that you have enough to buy anything you want, there's not much thrill in buying stuff. So, I now have an aquarium so big that we have to keep it in the living room, and it's got some very cool fish in it. Plus, I own just about every halfway decent video game that's come out. And The Scutters is one of the best-equipped bands around. Unfortunately, we still sound bad. But beyond that, just having stuff doesn't make me happy. So, I don't buy a lot of stuff.

Maddie's money is sitting in the bank. When she gets old enough, she's going to have her own foundation. She doesn't know about that yet. She's still thrilled that she has ten dollars.

Mimi and Ari thought they might become boyfriend and girlfriend now that Ari has stopped forcing himself to be so Ari-ish. Then they look at each other, laughed, and went back to being two of the three best friends who ever existed.

We're certainly more popular than we were back before we became three of the richest best friends who ever existed. Kids know who we are. They nod at us when they see us in the hall. We get invited to parties. But we can't tell how much of it is due to the money. So now we're popular, but it doesn't mean anything to us. The thing is, I think popularity is always like that: the reasons people become popular are too confusing and messed up to make popularity a way of telling anything real about yourself.

And what about the lottery itself? Because of all the publicity around my big win, the question of whether there should be a lottery got put on the ballot so that at the next election, everyone got to vote on whether the state ought to quit it. My father spent most of two months going around the state giving speeches against the lottery. On election night, we all stayed up late to see the results. And it was a landslide: The people of our state voted overwhelmingly to keep on having a lottery.

I was disappointed. But who am I to complain?

Thank You

Thanks first to our three children for being interested in books and stories.

Thanks also to those who read early versions and made helpful comments, including, Jerry Gasche, Staci Kramer, Alexandra Noss, and Michael Shook. A special thanks to Julianne Chatelain for her many, many suggestions.

A special thank you to Stellio LLC (stelliollc.com) for designing the covers and the layout of the book. It looks pretty good, doesn't it?